Also by Georgia Peterson

The Butterfly Sanctuary

The Stars Aren't Ready

THIS STORY CONTAINS content that might be troubling to some readers, such as suicidal thoughts and actions, child abuse and abandonment, postpartum depression, feelings of grief, drug use, violence and coarse language. Please be mindful of these and other possible triggers and seek assistance, if needed, from the resources at the end of the book.

First published in 2023

A catalogue record for this book is available from the National Library of New Zealand

Cover illustration by Kelly M. Carter

ISBN 978-1-99-117622-6

To all of those who keep trying,

Chapter One

People used to call me Joseph, but that was never my name. It was only because people thought I looked similar to Joseph Gordon Levitt. Well, mostly my teachers did when I attended school, which I no longer did. My name is Joel, and it is pretty close to Joseph, so people got confused. If I'm honest, I was just another average-looking guy that looked similar to Joseph Gordon Levitt, in my city, New York.

I was eighteen. I had brown eyes that Livvie used to tell me reminded her of chocolate. I had a soft New Yorker accent, and hair that was always a brown scruffy mess; I was past caring a while back. It covered up the scar on my forehead though. I also had a week's worth of stubble, dimples when I smiled, which I hardly did anymore, and an average nose. There was nothing special about me except, well, I planned to kill myself today.

Standing for what I hoped would be the last time in my room, I looked around. I wouldn't really call it *my* room. It looked pretty neglected, kind of how I felt.

I slid into some old sweats and threw on an olive-colored hoodie, a puffer vest, and an orange beanie, ready to brave New York's brisk, cold fall weather.

Underneath my hoodie was a homemade explosive vest. It's crazy what you can buy on the internet these days... and no one questioned me about the C4 in my shopping cart cause, like, it was all online.

It'd been too easy making a homemade bomb. The thought that anyone could do it almost scared me. But I was that "anyone" so what could I say.

I slipped the trigger button into my pocket and zipped it up, then walked out of my room. I couldn't help but stare at the door opposite as I closed my own behind me. Anxiety flared up inside me.

No sound came from inside the room, but I guessed my mother was sprawled out across the bed, high on whatever *delicious* drug she had chosen.

I pushed away my anxiousness and not another thought for my mother crossed my mind as I came out of the small hallway into the living area. It was a complete mess.

I stepped around the trash littered all over the floor and reached my bike by the front door.

I took one last look around. It felt good leaving. I would never be coming back and... well, that thought pleased me.

Carrying my bike down the steps of the run-down apartment complex, I then hopped on and started my trek.

I wasn't completely apathetic. I wanted to die, but I didn't want to die just anywhere.

Living in Brownsville, the East Side of Brooklyn for my whole life meant I'd grown up around drugs, crime and, it was one of the most poverty-filled areas in the city so it wasn't surprising I'd decided to leave it. I was only surprised that it had taken me this long to do it.

Looking up at the horizon, the sun was taking its time to rise, and the fog was dissipating slowly. The golden sunrays bounced between buildings, reflecting on the glass, and making it impossible to escape from. I didn't mind, in fact I actually welcomed it. It kept me warm as the icy fall wind whipped past me.

Fall in New York was always something else. Some days, it felt like summer and others, the winter chill dug its claws in. Those in-between seasons could be fickle.

Thousands of leaves swirled around me, and a fresh frost topped the ground, so it was pretty treacherous stuff, riding my bike on a slippery surface with a bomb strapped to my body.

I hadn't completely thought things through, but I wasn't going to risk going on any form of public transport. It was only an hour and four minutes to my destination anyway; I'd be all right.

An hour's biking wasn't much to me anymore. I'd grown up cycling wherever I needed or wanted to go. It was probably the only good thing that came from having parents like mine. I got my dad's old bike after he left us. I had to grow into it first, but I remembered the excitement when I could reach the pedals.

A similar excitement filled me now, and warmth from the sun radiated through me. Putting my head down, I pedaled faster to my destination.

Chapter Two

9:23 a.m.

Every inhale burned my lungs when I finally came to a stop. The chill turned my breath into tiny water droplets as I let it out in bigger exhales. My own personal fog.

I lifted my burning legs over my bike and stood beside it. Both calf muscles started spasming from the long bike ride. I held on to my seat and handlebars, waiting for it to pass.

After a minute or two, the spasms subsided and I took a long breath out. Letting go of my bike, it dropped to my side with a crash. I didn't really care if it got stolen or trampled on—I didn't need it anymore.

Unzipping my vest pockets, I carefully slid my hands in. The left pocket held the trigger. I curled my fingers around it, willing them to warm up.

Comfortable now, I looked up. Grand Central Station—one of the busiest places in the city, and the perfect place, in my eyes, to die.

It wasn't that I wanted to hurt anyone, the station just meant so much to me. *Livvie*. I shook my head, trying to escape from the memory attempting to grab my focus.

Staring up, above me was the station's grand windows, focusing on the world's largest Tiffany clock which had just struck 9:23 a.m.

Fellow New Yorkers bumped into me, breaking my train of thought. They hurled abuse my way for blocking their path, but I was used to it. I grew up in New York, after all.

The city never really stopped. People never had time to look up and appreciate what was in front of them. Everyone was more concerned about not being late on their daily commute.

I started getting pushed away from the clock by the herd of people surrounding me. Accepting it, I moved with them toward the 42nd Street passage to the station. There was no point fighting it—I mean, come on, have you ever heard of someone taking on a group of New Yorkers on their daily commute? That would be absolute madness.

I'd never really liked being shoulder to shoulder with other people, anyway, but it must've been the *push* I needed to get inside.

Walking down the ramp entrance, we turned left past the dining concourse, then the crowd basically popped out of the small corridor and almost fell over each other. I'd never dined in that concourse before, nor did I wish to.

I walked over to the wall to get out of the oncoming traffic. This was exhilarating. I squeezed my eyes shut for a second to rein myself in. Opening them again, I looked up toward the chandeliers. They kind of looked like balloons, leading the way to the main concourse.

Following underneath them, I stayed close to the wall to avoid getting bumped into.

The worst thing would be if my choice to die was taken away by someone simply knocking into me.

Turning left again, I headed into the main concourse. This place always took my breath away; the place amazed me.

Livvie's face attacked my mind, her memory blurring my vision. I couldn't get her out of my head as I stumbled toward the center of the main concourse.

The sun streamed through the big grand windows, bringing me out of my daymare of memories. I let it spread throughout my entire body.

My eyes cleared and noticed the window casting shadows all over the ground. I followed them and traced one up a wall, bringing my attention to the architecture. It was amazing. It was like a labyrinth of arches and pathways that all seemed to have a purpose.

Every time I walked into the station, I always found a new understanding of why it took ten years to build, which was still pretty fast for 1903.

My mind always wandered to the history of the building's architecture, whenever I went somewhere like this. I mean, how on earth did they make these pillars? Did they climb up there and pass buckets of concrete up, making it higher and higher? **It. Blew. My. Mind.**

Someone shouldered into me, and I dropped flat smack on my... ash. Livvie hated swearing, so now I have a built-in filter. When we were younger we made up our own cusses and used to shout them whenever someone else swore. We would say crab, shirt, fork, ash... It was mostly because we heard the real words so much at home, but even now... I couldn't break the habit.

"Watch it, dude," a passing man barked, sneering at me.

"*Me?* You're the one who bumped into me," I yelled back.

I carefully got up, my thumb now hovering over the trigger. Heads turned toward us, perhaps wondering if we were going to fight.

Of course, none of them knew I had a bomb on me.

"Oh, get outta here! Not everyone has time to daydream," he said, biting every word that came out of his mouth. I almost felt sorry for the English language.

"Still could've walked around me."

He turned away, and I couldn't help myself. I cussed him out under my breath.

He spun back around. "What did you just say?"
He pushed forward into my bubble, getting up in my
face. His breath smelt like he'd smoked a pack a day
since he was twelve. Tears swelled in my eyes again,
but now for a completely different reason.

"Your breath stinks," I said bluntly, taking a step
back. Snickers rang out around us. A circle had
formed, this was not how I wanted today to go.

"Wrong answer." He stepped forward again, ready
to take a swing at me.

I saw the punch coming, but knowing my future, I
let his fist hit my jaw. I could have stepped back, but
it didn't matter. My free hand flew out of my pocket
to grip the bottom of my face. Not a bad hit for a
scrawny little idiot.

"You chose the wrong guy to pick a fight with,
dude," I told him. It almost sounded like a warning.

"Oh yeah? How come? What you gonna do about
it?" he sneered.

"This," I said, taking my other hand out of my
pocket, trigger in hand.

A gasp rang out, voices talking over each other, as
my buddy backed away with his hands up.

"What the crab is that?" he asked. Of course, he
didn't actually say "crab" though.

"What do you think?" I turned in a circle, looking at
people's faces. "Yes, it is. It's a bomb, and you chose
the wrong guy to mess with. So, everyone leave if
you like… except you." I said turning back to the

man. Tears brimmed in his eyes now. Perhaps his breath was getting to him too.

"Come on, I didn't mean nothing. I was just having some fun," he told me.

"You call that fun?" I said, now stepping into his bubble. "You call that fun? Bull."

He started to tremble, the tears now streamed down his face.

Footsteps echoed around us, the place emptying. I heard security guards shouting at everyone to leave, walkie-talkies going off, and tables being flipped to use as cover.

Everyone was going into a frenzy, trying to get as far away as they could from this ticking time bomb of a conversation.

"Please…" the man whimpered. "Please, I'm sorry. You can't do this. I have my whole life to live. I'll be better, please just let me go."

"You would've beat me to a pulp if you'd had the chance, let alone anyone else that you bumped into today. Don't even lie to me." Disgust filled my voice.

"Please… *Please!* My wife served me with divorce papers this morning, and my mother just found out she has cancer. I'm sorry, *okay?* I didn't mean anything." He fell to his knees, his hands clasped together. "I feel like my life is falling apart, but I still have so much to live for… and… and so do you!"

He was an utter mess. I almost laughed at how he was acting. Was he for real? **People. Change. So. Fast.**

Chapter Four

9:24 a.m.

I opened my eyes to the unknown, almost too scared to see where I'd ended up. The first thing I saw were my shoes.

The sun warmed my back. My hands gripped something metal. Taking my eyes off my shoes, I looked to my left, gently releasing my hands. It was my bike.

No... I whipped my eyes upwards. Grand Central Station stood before me. I blew out a breath in complete shock and took a few steps back, dropping my bike in the process. I patted my pockets, searching for my phone and finding it in my trousers. My other hand continued to pat, slowing when I felt the bomb vest still there, under my clothes.

My phone screen reads: "October 27th, 9:24 a.m.". One minute after I'd arrived here the first time. This couldn't be real.

I swiveled around, crashing into the crowd that had dragged me into the station the first time around.

They didn't pass through me like I thought they might. I stumbled with them, noticing judging looks cast my way as my vision blurred. I felt like I was looking through a fisheye lens. Blinking rapidly, I tried to bring my vision into full focus. Voices echoed around me, telling me to move and some asked me whether I was all right, but my breath felt strangled.

Spinning on my heels, my arms flew out, trying to push off anything they made contact with. A few people tripped with me, yelling insults my way. I landed on my forearms and knees. I quickly turned myself over, moving backwards away from the crowd. My breathing quickened when someone leaned into my eyeline.

"Hey, sweetie, are you alright? Are you okay?" She went to put her hand on my shoulder, but I slapped it away. Her concerned face turned hard as she rose from her crouched position. She backed away from me mumbling something to the people behind her.

Everyone's eyes turned wild. Panic and confusion fought within me. It was too much. I raised my hand out to them in a *stay back* gesture. And that's when I realized the bomb trigger was facing palm out to all of them. Literally every single person was now looking at the trigger, their eyes trailing down the wire to where it disappeared into my puffer vest. They all started to run away from me.

I somehow turned my ears off to all the shrieks and yells, not wanting to hear them again. Everyone was muted but it didn't stop me from seeing their mouths open, their eyes wide with panic. They were all terrified, and if I was honest... so was I.

I rolled myself into a ball, thumping both sides of my head. *Why was this happening to me?*

"No! This isn't fair! No, no, no!" I yelled out in frustration. Tears boiled down my cheeks; I couldn't contain them any longer even if I tried. I didn't want to be here anymore.

"Please," I whimpered out. I put every ounce of strength I had left into my last movement. My thumb pressed down on the trigger.

Boom.

Chapter Five

Memories wrapped around Joel's mind again and there was nothing he could do to stop it. He opened his eyes, seeing white all around him. He heard a constant beating that was getting louder with every passing second.

The memories moved in a circle at lightning speed forcing him to stand in the middle. They blurred into another tornado of colors, lifting him up. The constant beating turned into a steady heartbeat, that sped up in a panic.

Joel blinked, and the colors slowed. Greens turned into grass and trees, the blues into the moody sky overhead. The yellow, orange and red turned into a playground. Then, the sweetest chocolate brown color with a flick of gold was looking up at him. Livvie.

He looked down at her. Her hair, bright as the sun, was stuck to her sticky ice cream-covered face. Her mouth was a soft pale pink, a completely different pink to her rosy cheeks. She said his name, trying to pull him with her.

"Joel! Joeeeeel, Joel, Joel, Joel, Joel," her little voice squeaked.

"Yes, yes, I'm coming," he felt himself speak. "Just let me wipe your face." He pulled up his shirt, rubbing the hem over her face. She dropped his hand and stood there, grumpily, while he got the remaining ice cream off, and pushed her hair behind her shoulders. She was so little—two and a half? Meaning he was six, almost seven.

Once he was done, Livvie grabbed his hand again, pulling him toward the playground. Joel lifted her onto a swing and started pushing her without even hesitating. She squealed, giggling louder the higher she got. Her little hands wound around the chains so tightly they turned white. Joel felt her happiness growing with his. He loved her so much.

He let the swing slow down and helped Livvie out once it came to a stop. She giggled some more before running off in the direction of the slide. She dodged through the rest of the kids in the playground, more quickly than Joel could.

"Livvie, wait for me!" he yelled. She was already halfway up the ladder to the yellow slide. He ran around to the front of it just in time to catch her flying out at the bottom. Scooping her up in his arms, he held her, smiling with her. She had a face full of mischief, and she tried to wriggle out of his arms.

"You can't run away from me, Livvie. I have to look after you, okay? We're a team," he told her, putting her back on the ground, still holding her hand.

25

"Team?" her face became clueless.

"Uhh… like Mommy, Daddy, me and you are all a team."

"Why?" she asked, her annoying why-phrase coming in strong.

"Because we are family," Joel told her. "Look, it's like when we play ball with Daddy in the lounge, and we have to get the ball past Daddy. We have to work together. We are a team," he said, hoping it made sense to her.

"Mommy never plays, so she's not in my team," she said, folding her arms over her chest in a grumpy matter. Toddlers and their moods…

"Mommy plays sometimes; she's just busy," Joel said.

"No."

"Yes," Joel argued back. She was right though— Mom usually ended the game, but he didn't want to admit to it.

"You and I are a team?" Livvie asked Joel.

"Of course we are. Always. Now, let's go down the slide together?" Joel asked, ruffling her hair. Livvie hit his hand away, grabbing it in her own and dragged him back to the slide.

Chapter Six

9:25 a.m.

There it was again—the station staring down at me, but now I felt as if it was giving me a disapproving look.

I couldn't die and now I was going insane, personifying a dang building. I dropped my bike to the side and pulled out my phone. Still October 27th, but now 9:25 a.m.

I turned around, noticing the crowd of morning commuters that had dragged me into the station coming my way, closer this time. I jumped over my bike in a hurry, moving out of their way. This was different. I felt some comfort in changing the events of the day.

I still knew how I wanted to end my day, but this time I felt anxious about it. Maybe I needed to do it in a different place or way?

Confusion took a grip on me as I wondered what I did wrong. Maybe killing myself was what I was doing wrong… but it was my choice. That's what I didn't get. It was my choice, but it was being taken away from me. The universe, someone, or something was taking one of my only choices away from me.

My confusion burned into anger, and it fueled me. This was **MY** decision. Why couldn't I just make it?

I turned away, breaking into a run and plowed straight into a stranger who also seemed like they were in a hurry. We bounced off each other, flying in different directions, feeling like we were in slow motion. I could almost count the freckles on her face before I landed with a smack on the ground. Her eyes clenched shut in shock, and her arms flailed out sideways, trying to break her fall.

My hands clenched as I tensed up on impact. Dust flew up around us, and I looked at her, staring back at me with eyes full of pain. She started to mouth "Sorry," but she never got to finish.

When I landed, my thumb had pressed down on the trigger button…

Chapter Seven

Joel's eyes snapped open. He fully expected to be standing in front of the station, but to his surprise, he was sitting on his childhood bed.

It was home to Joel, even though he never wanted to admit it. This is where he grew up; this is where Livvie grew up, even if it was a mangy old apartment.

He predicted the memory that was about to play out and tried to fight it. The memory was too strong; it felt like his eyes were being pried open, something forcing him to replay it. Replay the memory of when his life started to go downhill—one of the first "big" signs anyway...

He was seven and his three-year-old sister, Livvie, sat next to him, too scared to make a noise. She must have thought if she made a peep, the whole world would crumble.

Joel looked at his sister. He'd forgotten how sweet she looked at this age with her sandy blonde hair falling over her face and her cute rosy cheeks. He felt an internal sob rake through him.

She had a Finding Dory *comforter across her bed, but she mostly slept with him, in his bed, under his* Transformers *comforter.*

The walls were an ugly yellow, darkened in the corners due to mold making its way into their room. He had a framed photo of the two of them on a chair next to his bed, along with an alarm clock. There wasn't too much else to the room except for a pair of goodwill shoes kicked off on the floor, a dresser filled with their old clothes, and a few of Livvie's toys and drawings scattered around.

A loud bang echoed as if it was rehearsed, bringing him out of his thoughts. He wasn't sure why he felt like the memory could change. It was still playing out as if it had really happened. Livvie wrapped her arms around him, snuggling into his side, trying to escape what they both knew was to come.

His mother's voice boomed out, yelling at their father, who yelled back.

Joel moved off his bed, picked up Livvie and placed her on her bed. He wrapped the comforter around her and gave her clear instructions to stay put no matter what. Tears welled up in her eyes, which broke his heart, but he couldn't listen anymore. He had to go out there.

Now, Joel wished he never did. Maybe things would have turned out different if he hadn't.

He cracked open the door, looking down the hallway, before quietly stepping out, and shutting it behind him. He heard a whimper escape Livvie before

I walked up to the wall, giving in to the urge to try it out. I'd never done this before—it was a tourist thing, and I wasn't a tourist. This was my home. This was my city.

"I want to die…" I turned away from the corner I'd whispered into, but before I could walk away, I heard a reply.

"Are you okay?" the wall whispered back. I turned back around and placed my ear to it. There was the voice again. "Are you okay?"

Was I hearing things? I looked around. Who was whispering back to me? I couldn't see anyone except tourists milling around.

Did the voice come from a tourist? Why did it matter? I was going to blow myself up anyway. I wasn't going to stop until I succeeded.

I turned back to the wall and replied. "No."

"Why?" the voice replied.

"Life sucks—the usual."

"Change it."

"Change what?"

"Life," the voice came off as innocent.

It wasn't that simple. "I wish it was that easy," I replied.

"Why can't it be?"

"Because I've already made my mind up."

"About what?"

"I'm going to die today. I *want* to go out with a blast…"

"Please—" the voice began, but I'd already started walking away from the wall. I didn't want to hear them plead. I headed toward the Vanderbilt Hall entryway, when I heard the voice yell. It wasn't a whisper. It didn't telegraph off the wall like all the other replies. I heard them yell out.

"Come back!" A pause… "Please! Where are you?" A plea.

I watched people's heads turn toward the sudden outburst. I heard security walkie-talkies cut in and out, echoing between people. I heard people murmur, assuming someone was lost.

Finding a bench, I sat down to watch it play out. A security guard walked up to the owner of the voice; to her. She wore a flowy skirt with fishnet tights underneath, and a plain long-sleeve top tucked in with a coat over the top. An artsy girl, with her black hair done up in a clip. Her eyes looked panicked, like the most important thing she'd ever have to do was find me. But there was one problem: she didn't know what I looked like. She didn't know that I was only twenty yards away from her, watching and listening like everyone else.

"Are you alright, Ma'am?" a male security guard asked her.

"Yes, I'm fine, but there's someone who's not. I need to find them." Her head swiveled around, looking for me.

"Are you sure? What do they look like?" the guard asked.

"That's the problem!" she sounded exasperated. "I don't know. But he told me he's going to hurt himself!"

"How?" The male and female security guards glanced at each other like it wasn't the first time some erratic person had gone on a rant like this.

"At the whispering chambers. I'm serious. I'm not lying." Her face was set, determined. I almost felt bad enough to put my hand up and help her out, but I didn't.

"How about we go outside and have some fresh air?" The female security guard suggested. She placed her hand on the girl's back, trying to direct her out, but the girl pulled away.

"He wants to die! Now! We have to do something!" She really did sound crazy.

"Ma'am, please come outside with us." The female guard started to push her gently away.

"But what if he's planning to die here? What if he has a bomb or something? He said he wanted to go out with a 'blast.' We have to do something! Please!" She was hysterical now. So hysterical that the security guards seemed like they were starting to believe her. They didn't stop pushing her away, but I heard them talk into their walkie-talkies.

"Harold? Could you keep an eye out for any nervous commuters?" the male guard said into his radio. "We've just been told that someone might be planning to commit suicide. This lady here said something about a blast so keep an eye out. Over."

"Sure, should I evacuate? Potentially a bomb threat? Over," Harold said in reply.

"Uhh… I don't think so. Over."

"Okay. Over."

Sadly, nosey commuters overheard the conversation. Word spread like a virus, the word "bomb" repeating over and over. Footsteps picked up, yells rung out. People scare so easily.

I didn't move. I sat back and watched everyone. If the security guards saw me, I would definitely stick out like a sore thumb. I was the only calm one now, as everyone tried to escape the station because of a rumor. A rumor that happened to be true.

An old man stopped and grabbed at my arm to try to pull me to come with him. "Hey, son? You coming or what? Apparently, someone has a bomb!"

"No."

He didn't know that I was the culprit…

"What do you mean, no?" He took his hand off me. "You wanna die?" I couldn't bring myself to tell him the truth, so I made up an excuse.

"No, I have to wait for my sister," I lied.

"Oh… Do you want me to wait with you, son?"

Why was he being so nice? "No! No." I was too fast to answer and his expression changed. I doubted he believed me now.

"Well, I'll wait for you two outside, so I know you made it out safe, alright, son?" He hesitantly started backing away.

I marched into the station, looking like I was on a mission. The floor squeaked under my feet. This was the first time I noticed it. It looked like it had just been cleaned. Maybe the night before, when the station closed for two hours at two in the morning, they had probably decided to polish the floors. Too bad I was about to make a big mess everywhere. Oops?

A tourist bumped into me. "*Merde, désolé ma faute,*" he said.

Why... why do I keep getting walked into?

"I don't speak... whatever you're speaking." My hand moved out in front of me, leaving the trigger in my pocket. I felt bad for the guy, he seemed flustered. His face was red from embarrassment. His eyebrows pushed together, making them look thicker than they really were, and his nose stuck out like a signpost. He probably expected me to shout at him. Like, *I knew* New Yorkers came off as angry ashes, but most of us weren't. Most of us just had things to do and places to be. I had neither.

"Uhh... no English?" He waved his hands out to me, still looking petrified. He wore an iconic "I <3 NYC" T-shirt.

"It's okay, no problem," I said, turning my tone soft. He seemed to appreciate this and put his hands down. A smile started to show on his face.

"*Je viens de France,*" he told me.

"France... so you're speaking French?" I asked him.

"Oui, oui!" he said too enthusiastically. I was probably one of the first he'd met or walked into that had nowhere to be, someone who had time for a conversation.

"Cool! Well, see you around." I gave him a thumbs up and a wave, then turned around, walking away. My hands went back in my pockets.

"Non! Attendez, s'il vous plait pouvezvous aider," he yelled out to me.

I kept walking until I felt a hand on my shoulder. I tensed up immediately. "What? Dude, what do you want?" I asked, turning around to him.

"Aider? Help?"

"Help? You want *my* help?"

He nodded and gave me a thumbs up. He was delaying my initial plan, but he did look helpless, "Okay, sure. *Oui?"* I swear when I said yes in French, he almost broke out into a dance.

"Je me suis perdu."

"Dude, I can't understand you. Do you know any English?"

"Non, pas beaucoup. No," he said with such a strong accent.

"Okay, okay, great," I said, sarcasm thick in my voice. I took a shot in the dark, "Are you lost?"

"Oui! Yes!" All right, that was something. I let go of the trigger again and took my hands out. Palms up, I used them to signal "where?"

He took a tour guide from his bag—something he should have done earlier. He pointed to the Empire

State Building. It was walking distance away, so I wasn't sure why he was in the station.

"Oh! Easy, you can walk from here," I used two fingers and placed them on my palm, making the movement of walking.

"*Marche?*" he made a marching movement.

"March? Yeah, sure, I guess. Do you have any paper? Phone?"

"*Téléphone?*"

"Yes! *Oui!*"

He took his phone out of his bag. He should've been wearing his phone on him so it didn't get stolen.

French Guy unlocked the phone and handed it to me. I went straight to maps and zoomed out, showing him where it was. Not sure why he didn't do that by himself, but I guessed it could still be confusing.

I tried to explain to him that he should turn right once he was out of the front entrance, then walk to Bryant Park, turn left, and keep walking until he saw the building.

"Understand?" I highlighted the route on his phone, hoping he was smart enough to follow it.

I wondered how he had been getting around. Had he just been wandering in circles? It didn't matter, not my problem. I felt myself start to close off. I needed to get away from him.

"*Okay, merci. Je pense que je l'ai!*"

"Awesome, good luck!" I handed his phone back to him and gave him another thumbs up.

"*Merci beaucoup, merci!*"

I wasn't quite sure why he wanted to go there. Like, it was great and all—cool view from the top— but five people died building it. And at the end of the day, it was just an office building.

The Empire State Building had opened eighteen years after Grand Central Station.

The architecture sure changed a lot in those years; funny how I keep thinking back to architecture. Maybe if things had been different, I could have been an architect. Livvie always went on about the buildings here, Grand Central Station most of all. I loved learning all her random facts, and I haven't forgotten any of them.

It cost around forty dollars to even enter the Empire State Building. That was almost some people's entire wage for an eight-hour day at work—if you were a waiter or waitress being paid minimum, for example. Or double what you would get for three hours as a dishwasher boy… unless you had the best boss like I'd had in the past. *The past*. I didn't want to think about that. It was basically the main reason why I was going to go through with my plan.

Something about helping that tourist made me feel different, made me actually feel something for once. I was helpful. I helped someone. Something I needed when I was younger, something *we* needed.

We.

My thumb goes heavy on the trigger. *For Livvie.*

Chapter Ten

Laughter and kids' voices echoed around Joel. The sound bounced off the walls, making Joel feel like he was lying in a school corridor. The noise felt like it was aimed at him. It jumped around in his head, until he zoned in on a familiar voice. A familiar laugh. His dad's.

Joel's eyes bolted open as he reached the end of a yellow slide; his father catching him at the bottom. His own voice echoed in his ears, mixing with his dad's. Kids around them were laughing, squealing, all of them filled with the excitement of a playground. It filled Joel too. He could feel it even though he wasn't technically there.

It was the middle of summer, and they were in Central Park. This was his favorite area—the Ancient Playground. It was called that because it was based off an Egyptian art piece at the Metropolitan Museum of Art.

His mother was pregnant with Livvie, lying on a picnic rug.

Joel was four.

His dad hoisted him up and spun him around. There was so much light behind his father's eyes, so much light.

Joel never could have guessed that it would fade in a few months' time, after his sister was born.

His dad put him down and Joel ran off to climb the playground, ready to go down the slide again. He loved the rush it gave him, the wind in his hair, the urge to close his eyes as his heartbeat sped up. He loved slides as a four-year-old. He loved a lot as a four-year-old, including his mother.

His beautiful mom. She was the best. She gave awesome hugs, always knew what to say and made delicious mac 'n' cheese, basically the only thing a four-year-old cared about. She was great.

"Tony... Joel... Come grab something to eat!" Mom yelled out to them.

"We'll be there in a minute, Summer," Joel's dad replied before turning back to Joel. "How about one last slide before we grab some food, buddy? What do you think of that?"

Joel's arms went up with excitement as he rushed around to the steps, climbing them and going down the slide one more time. Dad caught him at the bottom again.

They walked hand in hand over to his heavily pregnant mom. She had set out their picnic lunch and was waiting for them to join her before she started eating. She had that pregnant glow about her that transferred to others.

Joel sat down and ate away at his sandwich,
listening in on their conversation.

"How do you feel, darling?" said his dad.

"I'm good. It is hot today, though. Could we head
home soon so I can take a cold shower?" Mom asked.

"Sure, anything for you."

Around them leaves rustled, and the kids still
laughed, making a soundtrack to their meal.

"What should we name her, Tony?" his mom asked.

"Don't worry about it, we will figure it out," Dad
replied.

"She's due in less than a month."

Joel could feel the stress coming off his mom.

"I know, honey. It'll be okay," Joel's dad reassured
her.

"We could name her after your mother?" Mom
suggested.

"What? Maggie?" Dad chuckled.

"Yeah? It's cute," she said, shrugging.

"Hmm, I don't think so," he told her.

"Why? What's wrong with it?" Mom almost
sounded offended.

"I just don't want her name to be Maggie," he said,
a note of finality to his tone.

"I'm the one having the baby, Tony. All you did was
the easy part."

Dad looked down at his food, seeming to chew over
his next words. "Summer, Summer, honey… please
don't be mad," he said.

"I'm not mad!"

Joel was a good kid. By now, he should have interrupted them. Instead, he listened… learning.

"Okay, okay. Look, we will think about it. Let's not rush it. She might look like a Jenny or a Hope for all we know. We have to wait until she comes out," Dad said.

"When she comes out? You make me sound like I'm an oven."

"Honey, you're my *oven. My smokin' hot oven. I love you. And whatever you want her to be named I—"*

"What about Livvie?" Joel finally interrupted.

His parents both looked his way, like they had forgotten his presence. He swore it wasn't always like that, but sometimes they both zoned out.

"Livvie? Olivia? Hmmm… that is quite nice, isn't it Joel?" Mom said.

Dad reached out and ruffled Joel's hair. "Joel and Olivia. I like that."

Joel wasn't sure why he said Livvie, though there was a girl he had a crush on in Pre-K called that.

Dad smooched Mom on her lips, and she kissed him back. He left a hand on her belly, holding it there.

Joel moved Dad's hand away and crawled over to his mother's tummy. He put his ear to it, something he had done throughout her pregnancy. Joel could almost hear his baby sister's heartbeat. The soft drum of it made him feel warm.

That was his baby sister in there, and Joel believed he was going to be her protector. A big promise for a little four-year-old.

*A **big** promise.*

Chapter Eleven

I screamed out, my ears still filled with her heartbeat.

I dropped to my knees, my hands rolling into fists as I punched the ground with all my strength. Over and over until I was exhausted. Until my hands were a bloody mess. Until all the bones in them started to crack.

I fell onto my back, lying on the ground, looking up at the station. The clock was upside down in my vision. No one dared to come near me, I could feel their footsteps creating big circles around me—as if I was a horse about to kick them.

I slowly lifted one of my barely functioning hands into my pocket, taking out the trigger. Squeezing it in my hand, a vibration stroked through me. I sniffled. Tears rained down either side of my face, pooling on the ground.

"I don't want to be here…" I whispered it.

"I don't want to be here…" I said it.

Chapter Thirteen

A crackling beat ripped through Joel. He felt his whole body twitch, then an immense amount of pressure dragged him down, willing him to start again, willing him to try again.

He couldn't open his eyes. He couldn't yell out. He felt paralyzed.

*Joel heard the same heartbeat rumbling in the distance, getting louder and louder as more pressure pushed him down. It was too much. It was **too** much. The funny thing was, he preferred this over the memories. Please don't let him remember...*

Chapter Fourteen

9:30 a.m.

My eyes bolted open, seeing the station. My breathing coming out in rasps. What was happening to me? I didn't understand. Why was it sometimes nothingness and sometimes memories? It didn't make sense. None of this made sense.

I dropped my bike to my side.

Was it because I was holding back the memories? Could it be me? I wasn't letting myself see them—was that it?

It didn't matter anyway. I still wanted the same outcome.

I checked my phone. 9:30 a.m. Only seven minutes since this all began.

I couldn't be bothered anymore. Even if I didn't die now, would I live to the next day? Questions filled my mind as I strolled into the station with the same commuters I'd seen every time. They were a little ahead of me this time.

even know this guy, and I felt like he could have so much to live for.

I felt like I was the innocent bystander this time around. I told myself to relax, and I let him hold it. He looked up at me, and we stopped fighting.

I let go of the trigger. **I. Let. Go.**

It would be his choice this time—my life in his hands.

I felt calm. I hadn't felt calm once today. Maybe it was just knowing that someone else wanted to die too—that someone else felt as bad as I did.

"Why?" he asked. He sat still, never once taking his eye off the trigger.

"Because I've started to regret it," I said.

Chapter Fifteen

"Isn't it just so cool?"

Her question bounced around in Joel's mind along with hundreds of footsteps. His eyes were closed, and he focused on the rumbling he could feel coming from the ground underneath him. He was stretched out; his palms face down on the floor.

"Joel?" she asked again, hitting him in the arm to get his attention.

He opened his eyes. The celestial ceiling in the station stared right back at him...

He turned his head away from it to look at the girl next to him. An eleven-year-old Livvie looked back at him. Her eyes were still big and brown, and she had freckles that scattered over her nose and under her eyes. Her cheeks still had a tinge of rose to them, and her hair the color of the sun was splayed out on the floor.

"I said, isn't it cool?" she asked again, giving him a strange look, "Were you even listening to me?"

"Yeah, yeah, of course I was," he replied, but he had no idea what else she had been saying.

Chapter Sixteen

9:31 a.m.

Regret.

The Oxford definition goes along the lines of: to feel sad, repentant or disappointed over something that one has done or *failed to do*.

I felt... I felt depressed. Why couldn't I die? Why couldn't I be up there with Livvie?

My shoulders sagged, and I looked down at my shoes. I stepped over my bike. I didn't remember dropping it. It lay fallen like my hopes.

Did I even have hope in the first place?

I didn't look up until the floor started to change— the dusty street sidewalk becoming the nicely polished ground of Grand Central Station. The commuters must have picked me up and transferred me inside, or did I just walk here by myself? I didn't know. I didn't even know whether I wanted to be here anymore.

I kept moving with the crowd. They walked me up the stairs to the second level and put me back down.

I looked up. Blues and golds lit up the room. The celestial ceiling never ceased to amaze me.

This was her favorite part of the whole station. Olivia's favorite part. Livvie used to go off on a tangent, telling me all these random facts about the station, like how they had to repaint it due to mistakes. Over the years the ceiling had been added to and changed, for better or for worse, I didn't know. Livvie always wished that she could have seen it when it was first opened. Whenever I brought her here, we always wished for a seat but there weren't any in this area. Instead, we lay on the floor.

Perhaps they didn't put any seating in the main concourse because people would have been too distracted by its beauty and missed their train.

"Whatcha looking at?" A girl's voice bumped into me at the same time as her shoulder. I finally tore my eyes away from the ceiling, away from the memories that I was beginning to drown in. I took a sharp inhale when my eyes landed on her.

She was gorgeous. Her honey eyes shone, as they looked up to the ceiling. Her brunette hair flowed over her shoulders. Her smile curved up on one side, making her look a little goofy. She wore a long plaid coat, with a gray hoodie, black jeans and black boots underneath it.

My thoughts darted to the idea of love at first sight, about it potentially being true. Butterflies raced around inside of me, making me feel a little queasy.

"You know, you're the first person I've seen looking up." She turned her gaze from the ceiling to me, her eyes locking with mine.

"You're beautiful," I blurted out, shocked at my own confession. She gave me a funny look but dismissed my random outburst.

"I always forget people from New York are so straight to the point." She turned her gaze back up to the ceiling.

"Sorry... uhh... I was lost in thought."

"Shall I call you lover boy?" she asked.

Already giving me a nickname.... should I feel special?

"You..." I paused. "My sister," I said, awkwardly. "Uhh... she loved it here." I pried my gaze away from her, returning it to the ceiling.

"That's sweet. I love it here too."

"Do you... do you want to lie down?" I had no idea why I was asking her that. How was I asking her that?

"Lie down?" she asked.

We made eye contact now. I felt a tingle start in my heart, something I hadn't felt for the longest time.

"Yeah, it's better to look at the ceiling that way. Ya know... doesn't hurt your neck as much," I said, adding a twang to my words for some unknown reason.

"... Sure. Makes sense, lover boy." She had already begun to lie down before the end of her sentence.

I joined her. We spread out like starfish, our feet connected and our hands less than an inch away from each other. She smiled. I smiled. *I smiled.*

Something clattered nearby. We both took our eyes off the ceiling, zoning in on the noise.

It was the trigger rolling out of my pocket. The stupid trigger. How could I have forgotten? I grabbed it quickly, shoving it back in my pocket.

Too slow. She'd already noticed.

I saw her go through a range of emotions, but none of them panic. How could I have been so stupid?

"My sister," I said, trying to distract her. "She and I would lie here for hours looking at the ceiling."

"This sister of yours, is she still around?"

"Uhh… no she's not."

"Oh. I'm so sorry to hear that."

"Don't worry about it." I cut her off before she could continue. She sounded genuinely sorry, but I just couldn't. It had only been five days…

The longer we lay there, the more people started to notice. I bet a security guard would come over soon.

"You know, it's okay," she said after a moment. She looked completely at peace, and I couldn't comprehend why, but then again, maybe she hadn't connected the dots as to what the trigger meant.

"What's okay?" I couldn't take my eyes off her. She was giving me a reason not to die, but as soon as I looked away, that would all vanish. She turned her head, looking at me, searching my face for something.

"To have a break, take time to heal. It's okay if you want to. Lots of people do," she told me.

"Have you taken a break before?" I asked and I almost regretted it.

"I've tried to in the past," she said, almost a whisper.

"Why?" I wasn't sure why I was asking. The conversation was heading to an awkward point, but I just knew I didn't want her to stop talking.

"I lost my Dad when I was around fourteen; he was my hero."

"Oh, I'm sorry." I looked away, not sure what to say. My eyes landed on the crab—the zodiac symbol for cancer. Livvie's favorite fact about this place was about a single brick up there. It was dark, dirty looking as if they had forgotten to paint it. She used to say how that was me, *one of a kind*. She meant it in the best way possible.

"Lover boy?" Her voice cut the memory in half.
"Mm?"

"You know why I said, 'I've tried'?" She shuffled a little bit closer to me, pausing to take a deep breath, "Because I kept thinking about all the people around me. The people who loved me. I knew they needed me; I knew Mom did. And I wanted to be there for them. I didn't want to do anything that would hurt them." She meant every word; I could tell by her tone.

"I don't have anyone to take care of anymore."

I looked at her again. I couldn't believe I was about to do this.

"Wait!" She reached out and grabbed my hand, a hint of panic now appearing behind her eyes. "I've only just met you, and I can't help but like you. I want to know more about you, but I assume that trigger leads to some sort of explosive?"

It sounded sincere, and she finally guessed right, but all I could think about was how it also came out as a plea. Her hand felt nice in mine. It fitted like a puzzle piece.

"What's your name?" I asked, ignoring her question. She could guess the answer herself.

"Ella," she replied. She sat up, moving closer, our legs now touching.

"I'm Joel." I squeezed her hand; I sat up too before I continued. "I don't have anyone. I want to be with my sister, but you're starting to change that for me in the little time we have been lying here. Except... I failed her." A tear escaped my eye. "My sister. I didn't protect her. It should have been me."

"Joel... I'm—"

"We used to lie here because it was her favorite place. You see the crab—the cancer?"

Ella looked to where I was pointing,

"You see that dark brick below it? She always used to tell me that I was like that. One of a kind."

"She wasn't wrong," Ella said softly.

"Livvie was one of a kind. She stood out in my world." I stopped talking and let go of Ella's hand. I grabbed the trigger from my pocket.

Ella moved with me, her hand resting around mine... around the trigger. I brought it out for us to see.

"Okay, okay," Ella said, I think fully understanding that the trigger meant there was a bomb.

"You should leave. Go live your life."

She didn't let go of my hand.

"Joel... Maybe this is what my life was meant to be. Maybe this is how I go out. How we both get to take a break," she said, almost half-heartedly. Ella's soul was as beautiful as she was.

"I'm so sorry. I don't know any other way. You would never love me once you knew me. I can never be loved."

I started to panic, to hyperventilate. I didn't know what was wrong with me. I didn't want her to die, but that would mean staying alive myself.

"Joel... Joel? Look at me."

My eyes were filled with tears, but I looked at her anyway.

Her face was soft. I could see the light bags under her eyes that I hadn't noticed before. I saw her properly this time.

"I want you to know that it's okay. It is okay," she said again, tears forming in her own eyes.

She was nodding, convincing herself. I looked into her eyes, searching them like she had mine. She was completely serious.

I didn't know how to feel. I looked away, staring at that single brick again. Maybe someone could be my one of a kind, again. I didn't know anymore. Fork.

"Okay."

Chapter Seventeen

A sickly, creamy yellow appeared in front of Joel. His hand reached forward, toward a grimy, silver doorknob. He was back at home.

He felt his hand twist the knob and the door clicked open. He scuffed the bottom of his shoes on the mat before stepping into the house. He felt himself tense up, something he'd done every time he walked in since his dad left them.

It was dark; the curtains were all pulled. He shouldn't say "curtains" since there was only one, covering the sole window which let light into their living area.

Everything was turned upside down—couch cushions thrown around, a lamp smashed into pieces. All their kitchen cupboards and drawers were open, and so was the small fridge. It had been shifted slightly to the right.

Joel flicked on the light switch. Nothing. Nothing happened. The power was out. Maybe that was the reason an emotional storm had exploded through their house.

Joel walked forward, making himself a path to the fridge. Bending down, an awful smell filled his nostrils. Everything he had scraped together with the little money he had—the milk, the ham, the butter— had all gone bad. He stood and kicked the door shut, frustration filling him.

"Livvieee?" Joel called out. She should have come home earlier than him, but there was no reply. He jumped over the upended trash can and sprinted down the small hallway to their room. He closed the door behind him and dropped his bag.

"Livvie?" he whispered softly, "It's okay to come out now, I'm here."

"Joel?" A little whimper came from his left, under his bed. He kneeled, moving some stuff out of the way, and there she was. His ten-year-old, little sister. Still looking like a four-year-old to him.

Her big, brown eyes stared at him. She looked terrified. She hugged a soft toy that they had found outside a thrift shop in a basket labeled "free". It was a little crab. Joel reached out his arms, pulling her forward. He hugged her, holding her tight, thankful she was okay.

"Are you hurt?" Joel asked. Livvie snuggled into his chest. He shifted around, leaning his back against the wall.

"No, I came home from school, and everything was tipped over. I went to see Mom, to see if she was okay, but she screamed at me to get out." A sob escaped Livvie.

"It's okay, take your time." Joel brushed her hair away from her face.

"Then, I hid under your bed like you've told me to do, and I heard her going berserk again. Why is she like that, Joel? Why isn't she like all the other moms I see at school? What's wrong with her?" Livvie looked up at Joel. She looked so confused and so miserable. He had never seen her eyes this way before. It felt like his world was ending.

No doubt her biggest wish would have been to have a "normal" mom. Joel had known there would be a time where Livvie started asking questions, and he hadn't realized she would start so young. She was only ten. And he was only fourteen. He didn't know how to explain why their mom was the way she was.

It wasn't their fault, but ever since Livvie was born, Mom had been different. She had mood swings. She was never interested in anything anymore, and Joel always heard her crying in the middle of the night. She never recovered from Livvie's birth. Something went wrong during the delivery, and she was left in constant pain. She blamed Livvie for that. She blamed Dad for giving her another child, and Joel for not helping out more, making more work for her. Mom was disconnected from everything and everyone.

And when she returned to work the doctors stopped prescribing her painkillers. They tried her on some other medication that was supposed to help her with her postpartum depression, but that just led her to another addiction.

Then she had found something much worse to numb her pain. She used to come home with the reddest eyes Joel had ever seen. For a while, he'd thought she was just tired, but he once saw her pushing a needle into her arm when he was only six, two years after Livvie was born. He hadn't known what it meant then, but when he got older, he figured out that his mom had been injecting herself with heroin, which was a type of opioid, a pain reliever.

Joel later found out that someone at her work had suggested it, to help her manage her pain levels and to help with postpartum depression. Apparently, everyone was using it as some sort of "reliever". Joel had overheard all of this in a heated conversation between his parents when he was younger.

He hadn't understood any of it at the time, but the words "heroin" and "postpartum depression" were burned, engraved, in his head. And ever since she started injecting herself, she had become more and more addicted. Dad had tried to fight for them, for the family. He had tried to find her support and get her help, but it had been too late. The best thing for her was to live in a permanent haze, to keep her pain away.

"I don't know, Livvie," Joel lied. He didn't think she would understand if he told her the truth, but he would have to tell her eventually.

Joel had heard about so many child abandonment cases at school, where the siblings got separated, so he never complained or talked about their home life to anyone. Joel's life would have ended if someone took Livvie away—another reason not to tell her the truth.

"I'm just gonna see if Mom's is alright, okay? You stay here," Joel told Livvie.

Joel knocked on his mom's door. The sound was barely audible over the music blasting from her room. His hand gripped the doorknob. He felt sweat trickle down his back, he was afraid of his own mother. He found strength, in the fact that he still loved her, and opened the door.

The smell inside almost made him vomit. It went up his nostrils, making itself at home through his entire body It was a mix between mold, bodily fluids, and vinegar. In that moment, he knew he would never forget that smell; it would be stuck with him forever.

The sight of the room added to his nausea. Takeout wrappers covered the floor, bedding was thrown to one side, and clothes were strewn everywhere. A dim lamp in the corner—the only source of light— illuminated a figure, an unmoving one, curled up into a tight ball.

He thought about closing the door and leaving her there, but as he stepped back, he hit something, someone—Livvie, right on his heels. Her hands screwed up into determined little fists, her face curious but afraid.

"I told you to stay in our room," he said.

"I want to see her too," she said.

"Livvie, it isn't safe."

"You're not the boss of me."

Joel let out a frustrated sigh. "Look, you can't come in. You stay in this doorway. Do you understand me?" This would no doubt scar her for life.

"But—"

"No buts. I'm serious, Livvie. Stay. Here." He walked into the room before she could argue back. He had to see if Mom was alive. Even if she was a piece of crab, he couldn't leave her like this.

He gulped down his fear and stepped over all the trash, making his way around the bed. He glanced back at Livvie, relieved to see she had stayed put.

His mom lay near the top corner of her bed, Joel hesitated. He looked down; there were a couple of used needles scattered on the ground, but mostly it was a number of little clear pouches which held Mom's gold. It looked like she had been shooting heroin into her system non-stop for who knows how long.

He bent over her, trying to hear whether she was breathing. She reeked of pee. He couldn't hear her breathing, so he slowly touched her arm. As soon as his fingertips made contact with her skin, she jolted alive as if his electricity had transferred to her.

She unscrewed herself from her tight ball and grabbed his arm pulling him in. She acted like a Venus flytrap, and Joel was the fly. He shrieked and pulled them back off the bed. Mom landed first, but she didn't release his arm.

Chapter Nineteen

Mom's screams and Livvie's pleas merged into one. They swirled in his head, changing volume from low to high. He couldn't open his eyes. He couldn't move. He was helpless. They were helpless.

The only thing he felt in his gut was that his fate, his life could never be changed. This would always be his story, his nightmare.

Chapter Twenty

The station left my vision as I fell to the ground. Sobs raked through me, causing jolts to rattle my entire body.

I was a horrible person. I was horrible for wanting to die when I should have been thankful for still having a life. I was a horrible, disgusting human being that didn't deserve to live.

Still kneeling, I let my breath come back. Maybe it was the station that caused all of this—the flashbacks, the memories, the not being able to die.

I stood up, heaving a foot underneath my weight; my broken, broken weight. I looked up at the station. Even though it may have been what was causing my problems, I still felt love for it. I still saw the beauty in it. I would never hate it.

I took one step back, then another, leaving my bike. I ran from it.

"This will be it," I repeated over and over to myself. "This is it."

"Yes, thank you so much, sir. You don't know how mu—"

"You haven't got the job yet. It's a trial," Dufty told him again.

"Right, yes. Yes, sir."

"Soap, brush, gloves and drying rack is here." Dufty opened a cupboard under the sink and pointed to everything. Only now did Joel notice the dishes next to him were stacked as high as him.

"Thank you, sir," Joel said.

Dufty nodded to them then headed out. Joel found the plug and started filling the sink up with hot, bubbly water. He heard Dufty move back into the kitchen with a chair placing it beside the bench and motioned for Livvie to sit.

"Sir...?" Joel asked, Dufty slowly turned around to face him.

"Yes, son?"

"You don't have a first aid kit, do you?" Joel asked. Duffy frowned. "What for?"

"We were biking when my sister slipped and cut her foot on the pavement," Joel lied... well half-lied.

Dufty sighed, making Joel think he regretted letting them come in. "It's on the shelf above you. Red box."

"Thank you so much." Joel was already moving to grab it. He had to get that nail out of her. With his arms up in the air, Dufty walked out before popping his head back in.

"Call me Dufty," he told Joel. Joel smiled and gave a firm nod. Dufty then left, properly going back to the front counter.

The first aid box was heavier than he thought, and he almost dropped it into the sink. Joel opened it and saw the two things he needed, antiseptic wipes and a bandage.

"Livvie, lift your foot up for me," he asked her.

She did as she was told, and he could feel her leg shaking in his hands. Gently he used the antiseptic wipe to clean around the hole. He wasn't even going to attempt to take the nail out, the thought made him gag.

"This might sting, okay?" Joel told Livvie.

He wrapped the bandage around her foot a few times, slowing every time he heard her wince. He put her foot down. He couldn't do anything else, though he wanted to so badly. Joel put what he used in the kitchen trash and placed the first aid kit back on the shelf. Kneeling in front of her, he cupped her face in his hands.

"I got you. Two hours, then we will go to the ER, okay?"

Livvie nodded, unable to find any words. Joel wiped away a tear with his thumb and rested his forehead on hers. They breathed in the same air before he broke their bond, he then put the rubber gloves on, and set to work.

*

She looked up. "How old are you two?" she asked suddenly interested.

"I'm fourteen. She's ten."

"Are you two okay?" she asked.

"My sister..." He choked on his words. "She stood on a nail and..." He stopped there. She didn't need to know the whole story but he also couldn't help but protect his mom, some habits were hard to break.

"Okay. Sure, kid. I'll call a nurse to have a look," she said, typing on her computer screen.

"Okay... okay, how much will that cost?" Joel asked.

"You have money?" She looked surprised. "Don't worry about that. Your parents' insurance will cover that."

Joel shook his head. "Will fifty be enough?" He had no idea how much anything really costed.

She made a face Joel didn't know how to interpret. "Just take a seat, and a nurse will be with you soon... What's your name, honey?"

"Joel."

"Joel... and your sister?" She raised her eyes from the computer screen, peering over the counter at them.

"Livvie—Olivia," he said.

A little less than five minutes later, a nurse called them over. Joel woke Livvie, and she dozily limped with them to a little medical bay.

"Can I have your foot, sweetheart?" the nurse asked her.

Livvie nervously tucked it under her chair. The nurse wore pink scrubs, and her hair was in a low bun. She sighed, not helping how tired she looked— exhausted more like it. Freckles covered her whole face and almost covered up the huge bags under her eyes.

"It'll be alright," Joel said, and Livvie reluctantly gave her foot to the nurse.

"Thanks, hun. Just a having a little look. It'll be over before you know it," the nurse said. It all went silent while the nurse frowned at the wound after undoing the bandage.

"We'll have to pull it out and give her a tetanus shot. I'll go get a doctor," she said looking up at Joel.

"Can't you do it? Please?" Joel asked hugging Livvie closer. He didn't really want anyone else seeing them.

"Yes, I can, I just want to double check it with a doc," the nurse said, her words final. She got up, taking off her rubber gloves and walked away from them.

A few minutes later the same nurse came in, followed by a short doctor who wore blue scrubs. Glasses sat on the end of his nose, and he rubbed his eyes, looking like he had only just woken up. The doctor glanced at the two of them. Curiosity filled his eyes before he shook it away, zoning in on Livvie's foot.

"Okay, okay, cool we are going have to pull this out," he said more to himself than the nurse. The

nurse nodded and grabbed a few things from behind them.

The doctor wiped this funny looking orange liquid on the base of Livvie's foot and she flinched away from his touch, squeezing Joel's hand tighter.

"Hey, kid, you're going to have to stay still. Could you get her to lie down?" the doctor asked Joel.

He nodded. "Livvie can you lie down, please? It'll be okay," Joel told her. She lay back on the bed, squeezing Joel's hand so tight he thought it was close to breaking. A few quiet minutes passed before the doctor started to speak again,

"Okay, all done, kid. I'll just bandage it up and then the nurse here will give you a tetanus shot just to be safe." Joel heard the nail clatter in a dish and looked down at the doctor who was wrapping Livvie's foot. Once finished, the doctor stood swiftly and walked out of their little area without a second glance. Strange.

"Olivia, could you sit up for me, honey? I'm just going to give you a shot to keep you safe, okay?" the nurse asked, bringing Joel's attention back to her.

Livvie sat up slowly, still squeezing his hand. She turned her head and whispered into Joel's ear. "I don't want to be like Mom."

When had she seen Mom doing drugs? He thought to himself. He shook the thought from his mind. "You're not. She's just giving you some medicine," Joel whispered back, hoping the nurse couldn't hear them.

"Right! All done! Try to stay off your foot for a few days, and I'll get some antibiotic cream. You need to put on it daily. I'll give you some bandages to re-wrap it if you need to," she said more to Joel than to Livvie.

They both thanked her and he helped her hobble back to the waiting area. He left Livvie there and walked up to the front counter.

"What do I owe you?" he asked the Mexican lady.

"Nothing, Medicaid will cover it."

"Medicaid...?"

"It's a program that helps with medical expenses for people like you who don't have insurance and can't afford the bills. Speaking of that, I'll need you to look at these forms, and I think someone wants to talk to you and your sister," she said like it was no big deal.

"I know what it is, I just..." Massive red flags went off in Joel's head; he did not want to talk to whoever it was that said they were coming. He was basically trapped. How was he going to leave without them noticing?

"But I can pay. I have fifty bucks if that's enough?" he asked her, trying not to sound like he was about to make a run for it. He pulled the cash from his pocket, but she looked at it like he'd just offered her Monopoly money.

"It's not, I'm sorry. But it will be covered; just have a look at these papers for me?" she said slowly standing.

"Okay, thanks, bye." Joel whipped around, rushing to Livvie. He snatched her up, and she wrapped herself around him again.

The Mexican lady came out from behind the desk, and he saw her gesture to a security guard. Joel locked his arms protectively around Livvie, and then he ran straight out the front door before anyone could catch them.

Chapter Twenty-Two

9:34 a.m.

I barely noticed my bike clattering to my side. A hospital smell filled my nostrils. Sunlight hit the station's windows, reflecting it back at me. This is the first time that, had happened, or at least, the first time I'd noticed it. I dragged my feet toward the station, entering it for the *tenth time?*

The universe obviously didn't want me anywhere else, and if I'm being honest with myself, this was the only place I wanted to be.

I sat on the closest bench, happily moving out of the way of the ongoing foot traffic.

I watched everyone pass. They all seemed like they had a reason to be here. Technically I did too, but I didn't know how to end the horror of this cycle I was in. It was like there *was* no end. Was I doing it wrong? Was I not allowed to die by explosion? Was that the reason why I couldn't die? It's not like I wanted to take other people with me... but then why had I chosen the bomb vest?

At the beginning, I hadn't cared. I didn't care about anyone, and I said I didn't care about myself either, but I think I was lying. I did care. I wanted to be selfish. I *did* want to take people with me. I thought that they didn't deserve to live because of how life had treated me, but it wasn't their fault.

Maybe it was just today, maybe I could hack the system. The day did have to pass eventually…

I grabbed my phone out from my pocket and looked at the time. It was 9:40 a.m. Only seven minutes had passed. This was going to be a long day.

I sat for a little longer on the bench, then decided to move with the crowd to one of the little boutique coffee places. I ordered a small coffee, unable to afford anything else, and waited in line to be called. A few minutes later someone called my name.

"Joel? Small coffee for Joel?"

I don't know why I'd expected it to take longer than it did. It was literally grinding beans and letting boiling water seep through them. A plain-Jane black coffee. Nothing to it. Just like me. Except that I was still carrying a bomb on my chest.

"Joel?" the voice called again.

"Yip, here, sorry. Was in my own little world." I moved out of the line to the side where they were handing out orders.

"I do that sometimes too! Enjoy your day." The girl pushed the coffee forward and turned around, going back to her next order. Before she did, I read her name tag. Livvie. Her name was Livvie.

Her hair was up in a messy bun, and she had big circle glasses that framed her small face. She wasn't exactly tall, just around average height. And for some reason, the whole coffee maker and waitress look suited her.

In my head I told my hand to take the coffee and walk out the door, but the movement felt robotic. Jagged. My hand finally gripped it, and I started to swivel around.

"OH! Sir! You forgot the lid! Sir?" Livvie yelled after me.

I stopped. I hadn't even noticed that there was no lid. It was the norm in coffee shops here—they would hand you the open cup, so you could add sugar or whatever you wanted, then grab your own lid. It saved the employees time, and it also let you have what you wanted. I was only ordering a coffee to keep myself awake for the next fourteen hours.

Suddenly, she was there in front of me, holding out a lid for me to take.

"Here you go!" she said.

"Uhh, thanks."

"Welcome. I would hate to spill coffee on my own clothes so I wouldn't want it to happen to anyone else," she said.

"Are you assuming I'm clumsy…?" I asked her. It came out more aggressive than I meant it.

She backed away immediately. "No, no, sorry, sir. I was… I was just thinking you'd want a lid. I didn't mean to offend you in—"

"Because you're right! I am clumsy," I cut her off, trying to make up for my comment.

Her eyes flickered with relief, and a small smile spread across her face.

"Right," she laughed. "I better go back to work. Here's your lid." She handed it to me but didn't make a move to back away anymore.

"Thanks, yeah, have a good day." I took the lid. She still didn't back away. Why was she looking at me like that?

"Are you alright, sir?" she asked.

How on earth could she sense that I wasn't okay?

"Yes, I'm fine… thanks for asking." I tried to move past her, but she stayed put, blocking my way. She crossed her arms and leaned her weight onto one leg. A motherly look came over her.

"Are you sure? I'm just getting this weird feeling all of a sudden that you aren't."

"That's just a silly feeling," I told her.

"Sir?"

"I'm fine. Honestly. Look, they need you back there. You better help them out." The words rushed out of my mouth, and I pointed back to her work colleagues.

"Are you sure? I can take my lunch break and we could talk?"

She was being so nice, I almost couldn't handle it. "I'm a total stranger? Why would you do that?"

"Why not?"

"Livvie…" It sounded weird coming out of my mouth since it wasn't *my* Livvie. I watched her look down to her name tag, surprised. She obviously forgot that she was wearing it. "I'm okay."

"Mmmhm," she said, clearly not believing me.

"Livvie was my sister's name," I blurted out. I couldn't help myself.

"Oh—" She went to say something else, but I cut her off again.

"She's not around anymore…"

Her hands flew up to cover her mouth in shock. "I'm so sorry. I never should have said anything," she said, slightly muffled behind her raised hands.

"Don't be. It's not your fault. It's a really good and caring name," I said.

She nodded, awkwardness twitching off her. Her eyes darted back to the kitchen.

"Don't worry about it," I said again. "Thanks for the lid."

"I better head back…"

"Yeah…"

"Sorry again, sir."

I nodded, and she walked past me. Before she started making another coffee, I called out to her.

"Hey, Livvie?"

Her head shot up.

"Keep listening to your feelings. We need more people like you. Make the world a better place one act of kindness at a time, yeah?"

It had been seven hours since my last human interaction. I'd stayed clear of other people just in case they also got "feelings" that something was off about me.

I'd been walking, exploring the station. It never seemed to end. Unsurprising, considering it was the largest train station in the world, but still forty-eight hectares was crazy. How on earth had they made it that big, and why? That question had been on my mind for the last hour as I walked past platform after platform and archway after archway. Chair after chair. Trash can after trash can. The list continued. I probably should had done something productive like counted how many trash cans there were so I could report the overuse of trash cans in the station. The poor cleaning staff. I bet they didn't even empty them every day when there were so many.

I was becoming delusional. I shouldn't have had that coffee. Looking around, I found a bench close by and sat down again. This time, I didn't care whether I got comfortable. If my body wanted sleep, I was going to let it sleep. What else did I have to do?

*

A bell echoed above me, waking me up. It rang through my ears, my eyes, and my mind, jolting me awake.

It was no longer day. The clock had just struck midnight. It was midnight. I'd finally made it to a new day! *See you soon, Livvie.*

I stood up, stretching my legs, clicking my back, and adjusting to what now felt like a twenty-pound weight on my front.

The station lights had dimmed, and noises came from somewhere out of sight, putting me on edge. I walked forward, already feeling someone shadowing me. Nothing about this felt right.

My heart started to race, an invisible hand gripped my throat making my breath falter with every new step. What was happening to me?

My hand screwed around the trigger, feeling like someone was forcing me to press it. This is not how I wanted it to go. I wanted to do it, but I didn't want to be forced. It was *my* decision.

My hand cramped and I let out a little shriek. My eyes rolled back into my head as I balled up. I let myself go limp. For the first time out of the many it felt wrong to be dying, like it was no longer the answer.

Chapter Twenty-Three

"C'mon, Joel, put your shoes on," Mom called. She was waiting outside the front door for Joel. He had just finished breakfast but found his shoes a challenge. He was only five years old.

"Coming, Moooommm," he called back to her. They were going out together, he wasn't sure where, but it was just him and Mom.

Dad was currently asleep across the couch. It had been a long night for the both of them. He'd heard Dad get up more than eight times for Livvie, and he overheard Mom and Dad saying she might be teething—her first tooth. Joel didn't really understand why Livvie was crying so much about it. She should be excited because then she would be able to eat proper food. Proper food meaning Mac 'N' Cheese!

"Joel? Are you coming?" his mom called again.

Joel finished doing the Velcro straps on his shoes and ran toward the front door. He caught up to Mom, who was halfway down the stairs. He jumped off the last step next to her, and she held out her hand for him to take, which he did happily. She smiled down at him. She was so beautiful.

Her eyes were green with little flecks of yellow in them, and they had a faint red rim around the edges. Her smile was fighting to reach her eyes. Freckles scattered across her cheeks and over the bridge of her nose. Her straight brown hair flowed over her shoulders. She was wearing a summer dress with a strawberry print. Joel thought she was the most beautiful thing he knew of, apart from Livvie.

"Mommy?" he said as they started walking down the street, still hand in hand.

"Yes, Joel?" she asked, her voice soft, motherly.

"I love you so much," he said. She almost faltered in her step and her eyes glossed over.

They reached the corner of the street where they usually crossed, but Mom bent down to Joel instead, kneeling in front of him. She did it slowly, like the action made her uncomfortable and sore. Her eyes were still shiny, and her cheeks had gained some blush to them. She reached for his other hand and held them both.

"Thank you, Joel. You don't know how much that means for me to hear. You are the best boy I could ever ask for. Never change, okay?" A tear made its way down her cheek.

"Why are you crying, Mommy?" Joel asked. He furrowed his brows together and pursed his lips. Had he made her sad?

She let out a little laugh and let go of Joel's hands. Mom cupped his face in her hands. She sniffled before leaning her forehead to his. Joel started to smile instantly. They knocked noses, and Joel broke out into a fit of laughter. He was always the most ticklish whenever Mom did this.

Joel moved away from her, but it was too late. She already had him in her grasp. She started to kiss him all over, making Joel erupt into more laughter.

"Mom! Mooommm," Joel said, hardly audible in between breaths.

His mom stopped kissing him, but she still hugged him tight, almost as if she was saying goodbye to him.

"I love you too, Joel. I always will," she said.

Standing up slowly, she grabbed hold of Joel's hand again and ruffled his soft brown hair. Joel looked up at her, smiling, and she smiled back. It reached her eyes that time, but they still had a shiny look to them.

Chapter Twenty-Four

9:35 a.m.

"What just happened?" I said out loud as soon as I restarted.

I stamped my foot in frustration. Was it me? I just wanted to be with Livvie. I just want to be up there, in the stars, with Livvie.

Livvie once said that we turned into stars when we died, and I was pretty shocked with that statement—that she was talking about dying, but she was at that stage where she was figuring stuff out and curious about death. I didn't quite believe her, but I always went along with any idea she had.

Out of the sixty-seven million people that walk through this station annually, another random fact I learned, courtesy of Livvie; I just had to be the one that couldn't leave.

I walked in once again, taking my sweet time while the never-ending commuters worked their way around me. I decided to make my way to the dining concourse. Passing the whispering gallery and up the escalator I went. Marble, shimmers of gold, and elegant lights greeted me along the way. This was a place I did not look like I fitted in, and it was not one that I could afford either.

I took out my wallet, and I was surprised to see that I had the same amount I'd had before purchasing the coffee. I shouldn't have been surprised; I just thought that maybe the universe would happily take my money instead of me.

Walking up to a counter, I suddenly felt nervous about the curious glances of other customers. Everyone knew I didn't belong here. A worker then greeted me. He was dressed in a red waistcoat, with a white, long-sleeved shirt underneath and pinstriped pants. His hair was waxed back, making his face look more pointed than it probably would have looked normally.

"Hey, I—"

"Here's a menu of the things you might be able to afford." A snarky comment from a snarky face. His face. Pissed. Me. Off.

"I was actually going to ask whether you made cream cheese bagels... I don't want none of this trash," I said, and shoved the menu back at him.

Surprised with my reply, he moved the menu back to his side and nodded.

"That'll be eight ninety-nine,"

I threw ten bucks across the counter and moved out of the line.

The same worker brought the bagel to me about two minutes later. "Here you go," he said, immediately walking away.

"Could I have some napkins please? Gosh the service in here…" I yelled, loud enough for people nearby to hear me. He hurried back with a few napkins, slapping them down in my hand.

"Not cool, dude," he told me.

"Don't assume people's value through their choice in clothing or appearance. You never know, you could have just served the next president of the United States." My fingers curled around the napkins, and I left him there speechless to go find a seat. I wasn't going to let him ruin my mood when I was eating one of my favorite foods.

Looking around for an available seat, I noticed an elderly lady sitting in a booth alone. She had her cup, saucer, a little teapot, and some type of cake in front of her. I walked over, curious as to what her story could be.

"Ma'am? Hi, sorry, is this seat taken?" I asked hesitantly.

"No."

Blunt. I tried again.

"Can… can I sit?" I asked.

"Sure," she said, but nothing else.

"Thanks."

"What's your name?" she asked in a transatlantic accent with a twinge of New Yorker. A gold watch, which looked centuries old, wrapped around her wrist. She wore pearls—a necklace, pearl earrings and a pearl ring.

A plain, but no doubt cashmere cardigan wrapped around her shoulders. And it looked like her hair had been styled recently. The most important thing was that she had gentle eyes, even if she was a picture of wealth.

"It's Joel, ma'am." I felt obliged to shake hands, so I offered mine. She looked at me and then to my hand. She gently took it and gave it just one shake. One, firm, blunt shake.

"You don't have to call me 'ma'am', Joel. Call me Carol."

"Nice to meet you, Carol."

"Same to you," she said.

I unwrapped my bagel and took a bite. I could still feel her watching me so I looked back up.

Her eyes studied me, inquisitive. "What are you wearing?" she asked.

"A sweater?" I said quickly. Too quickly.

"No. What's underneath it, Joel?"

I felt like her naughty grandson, from the tone she used.

"A shirt," I said.

"Stop shirting with me Joel." She actually did swear, causing me to internally gasp. *Carol!*

"What's that bulge in your pocket?"

I looked down. The trigger in my pocket was basically outlined through my jacket fabric.

"It's... it's not what you think it is." Panic rippled through me.

"Joel, the only way to make us both comfortable is to tell the truth."

I shyly took a hand off my bagel and reached into my pocket. Bringing the trigger up to the table, I gently put it down.

"I'm sorry," I said.

"It's okay, Joel," she said, reassuringly, like it was totally okay that there was a bomb trigger in between us.

"How did you know?"

"A boy your size, at your age, doesn't normally have a bulge like that on his stomach."

She had a point.

"And judging by the look on your face, I guess I'm the first to say so," she added.

"Yea, you're right. Why aren't you worried?".

"There's no need to be worried. I've lived through a lot. I'm ninety-two for heaven's sake."

So, she did have a story.

"You don't look anywhere near ninety-two," I told her. *Kiss-ash.* She chuckled and took a sip of her tea. I took another bite of my bagel.

"So... does that mean you were alive during World War Two?" I asked her.

"Yes, I was." She sighed.

I could tell she felt obliged to tell her story, so I sat patiently waiting for her to start. It wasn't every day I got to talk with someone who was alive during a major historic event.

"Where do I start?" Carol asked.

"Wherever you like," I said, spreading my arms out wide.

"Hmm... suppose you're right, boy," she said with a small smile. She took another sip of her tea and then cleared her throat. "I wasn't alive during the First World War, thankfully," she said, pausing.

I wondered if she was waiting for me to agree with her.

"I was only nineteen when America joined the war in 1941; it was after the attack on Pearl Harbor. That was a dark day for our country. I can still remember the horror plastered on my mama's face when the news came across the radio." She paused again, her eyes seeming to cloud over from the memory.

I put down my bagel and reached across the table, giving her hand a little squeeze before pulling back. I wanted to show her that I was there, reliving her memory with her. She sniffled and let out a little laugh before she continued.

"Yes, anyway I joined as a nurse once I was twenty-one which was two years before the war ended. I mostly worked in field hospitals during my time, but I saw some horrendous things. Men with their limbs blown off... men dying without seeing their loved ones before going. It was tough."

"Shirt, I'm sorry. You don't have to continue. Do you want me to leave?" The bomb strapped to me was making me itch with guilt.

"Don't be sorry, boy," she said, the bomb didn't even bother her. "After the war ended, I came back here, to New York. My family were, surprisingly, all alive. I was twenty-three. I decided to keep working as a nurse at a hospital here. I watched my two younger sisters get married off and start their own families, but I never found anyone. There were flings, but nothing that meant I wanted to spend the rest of my life with someone." She paused again, taking another sip of her tea. "I guess I felt guilty. I dreamt of those poor men dying every night for years. They had no one, and I thought it would only be fair if I joined them." She stopped and looked at me across the table.

"But why?" I asked.

"I guess it feels like some sense of duty, but that doesn't mean life has that plan for me. I already decided that I'm not going to bother trying to convince you not to blow us up, Joel. I almost feel guilty that I'd rather go out with someone, with you, than completely alone."

"I guess I understand why you are so calm about all this now," I said sheepishly.

"Don't worry. I had an adventure of a life. I was alive during Martin Luther King Junior's time for heaven's sake. I've been alive for probably all the history kids get taught in schools these days. I'm not

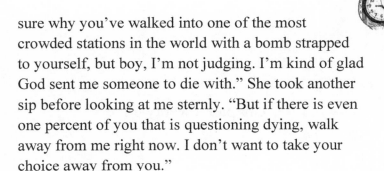

sure why you've walked into one of the most
crowded stations in the world with a bomb strapped
to yourself, but boy, I'm not judging. I'm kind of glad
God sent me someone to die with." She took another
sip before looking at me sternly. "But if there is even
one percent of you that is questioning dying, walk
away from me right now. I don't want to take your
choice away from you."

"I can't believe you're so okay with this, like, you
should be screaming and running by now," I told her.

"I'm ninety-two, I can't get up that fast. I miss my
mama and pa, and I think you're missing someone
too, aren't you?" Carol asked, hitting the nail right on
the head.

I only nodded, giving her a small grimace. Was I
that transparent? I wanted to thank her for the life she
lived, but I couldn't form any words. Carol reached
over to my hand, and she squeezed it, like I had hers.

"It's okay. I'm ready if you are. Better to go out
together than alone," she said.

I couldn't stop the tears that were filling my eyes. I
followed her old, wrinkled hand up to her face. She
had a small smile and the gentlest, softest eyes.

I should have run away right then, like she told me
to. I wasn't sure why I didn't want to die this time,
but for some reason, I thought that it wouldn't be so
bad to restart again.

Chapter Twenty-Five

October 23rd, 2008
Five days before

It was a Thursday. Joel was eighteen. He'd dropped out in his last year of high school because he could no longer afford to waste his time on what they called a "great" education.

Working full time at Dufty's, earning and learning as much as he could was way better than school could have been. He helped out with the cooking, waiting tables and the coffees.

Making coffees was probably his favorite thing, he liked the smell of the grounds and liked the power of being the person that gave the customers what they needed in the mornings.

Dufty was also getting older. He moved around more slowly than when Joel first met him and had even given Joel keys to the coffee bar, where on rare occasions, Joel was asked to open or close. It gave him a sense of purpose.

Livvie was his other purpose. He would work day and night for her. She was only fourteen and she had so much to live for.

He still made her attend high school, but she was often sick, catching every cold and flu out there. She'd been keeping up with school through the few library and textbooks Joel could get for her.

Joel wondered if it was the damp house making her sick... or the mold, or the constant stress. He even thought about that nail. Could she have caught something from it, despite the tetanus shot? Maybe he should have stayed and talked to the social worker at the hospital.

Joel hadn't been back to the ER since that night, but the way Livvie was going, he might have to if she continued to be as sick as he left her that morning. She had gotten so little, and she was so skinny lately. Being sick had put her off food since she kept throwing it back up.

When Joel went to the library on his lunch break to get Livvie more books, he also spent time reading brochures about the flu. The professionals said the flu can turn into pneumonia which he hoped wouldn't be the case. He'd felt his nerves prickle at the idea that Livvie might not get better.

Eight hours later he slipped out of work, exhausted. Dufty had told him to go home and come back the next day.

"Boy, you look like a zombie that has been alive since dinosaurs were a thing. Go home," he'd said.

All Joel could think about was that he probably looked like his mom, so with that, he did what he was told and left.

Biking home, he decided to leave his bike chained below the damp-looking apartment complex instead of bringing it inside. Joel trudged up the steps and lay a hand on the doorknob, shaking himself out of his haze. Opening it, he was greeted by no one, as per usual.

He closed it softly behind him and walked down their small hallway to the room he shared with Livvie. Before going inside, he opened his mom's door.

Her curtains were drawn, and it still reeked in there. She was thankfully asleep. He wondered whether she was starting to grow mold, considering the only time he had seen her leave her room was to get more drugs. He didn't know why, but he felt obliged to look after her, even if she was slowly killing herself. He was surprised she wasn't dead already... He left twenty bucks on her dresser before closing her door and backing into his own room.

His and Livvie's room was the complete opposite— light filled it. Everything was clean and in its place. It was their own little sanctuary. Livvie was reading a book, lying in what was left of the sun like a cat. She had balled herself up so small that she almost looked like a little child. He smiled at her and grabbed a change of clothes, deciding to go have a shower.

Afterwards, he slipped back into their room and sat on the other bed. He looked around their little home. It had drawings pinned up on the walls, Livvie's soft teddies, study books and homework on the floor; it wasn't much, but it was all theirs.

Livvie looked up from her book and started to uncurl herself. She looked so fragile, and she took her time, stretching each limb.

"Joel?" she whispered. Joel moved to her side immediately. Alarms went off in his head. She looked far worse than when he left her this morning. She'd had some color to her cheeks then, but now she was paper white. Weakness took over her, and she flopped forward towards Joel. She felt hot to the touch. A crackling cough went through her as she heaved another breath in.

"Livvie? Livvie?! Right, come on, let's get you to the hospital."

She moaned against him as he rolled her onto her back.

"Nooo," she whined.

"It's not an option," Joel said.

"I don't remember Dad," she said randomly.

Joel felt shock move through him. How could she not remember Dad? "What are you talking about, Livvie?" he asked. She was becoming delusional.

"Is Mom nice? I can't remember what she looks like?" Confusion took hold of her face.

"Livvie…" Joel said, pity lacing his tone.

121

"Why can I only remember you?" she said, no accusation in her voice.

"Because I'm always with you. Now c'mon." Joel struggled to put her shoes on. She was scaring him.

"Because... you're one of a kind," she told him. Joel hurried to get her dressed. He could feel his panic rising.

"I want pizza," she said.

"We are going to the hospital," Joel reminded her.

"No, I am not." She raised her hand to her face and coughed again, hard. He noticed her wipe her palm on her shirt, a shiny mucus residue left behind.

"Livvie, please." He had read the warning signs of pneumonia earlier and she was currently showing all of them. Maybe she'd been fighting that instead of just the flu like Joel suspected.

"Joel, I want pizza. And I want to lie in Central Park and stare at the stars," she told him.

"Livvie, you're sick."

"For once, Joel, let me have what I want," she said, as if Joel's whole life hadn't been trying to give her just that. Livvie looked at him with her big round eyes. She was on the edge of tears.

"Fine. But straight after, we are going to the hospital. Take some Tylenol before we go, though, to bring your fever down." Maybe the food would help. He didn't want the hospital staff thinking he didn't feed her.

He brought her a glass of water and two tablets, then found his warmest coat, wrapping it around her.

He also put an orange beanie on her head. He reached out his hand for her to take, and with his help, she slowly made it down the stairs to his bike. She gingerly got onto his front handlebars, and he hopped on the back. Joel moved the strap he had tied in between the handles to rest behind Livvie's back. It helped her hold herself up while he biked. They then set off slowly toward the pizza shop, as careful as Joel could go.

Ten minutes later, they arrived outside of Johnny's Pizzeria, Livvie's favorite place to go. Joel helped Livvie get off his bike, and they walked in. Johnny, the chef, turned around and smiled broadly at them.

Johnny was large—large in height and large in weight. He was almost completely bald except for the thickest eyebrows Joel had ever witnessed on someone's face. They almost made him look cartoonish which Joel struggled to wrap his head around. He had the thickest New Yorker accent Joel had ever heard. Johnny knew how to cook the best pizza Joel and Livvie had ever tasted.

Ever since Joel started earning his own money, he would try to take Livvie here once a week. From the very beginning, he could tell Johnny never charged them the full amount for their food, and Joel was very thankful for that.

"Johnnnnnyyyy!" Livvie yelled to him, before spluttering into a little coughing fit.

"Livvie! Joel! My favorite sibling pair! What can I do for you two today?" he asked, smiling at both of

123

them. His eyes shifted to Joel's, and he could see the concern in them.

"I want it all Johnny—the cheese, the pepperoni, the wholeeee deal. You know what I want," Livvie replied cheekily. She sure had found some energy again.

"Coming right up, your majesty!" Johnny replied. He turned around and gave a yell to his other cook. "One pepperoni and one Hawaiian even though pineapple doesn't belong on pizza!"

"You and your opinions. It tastes good," Joel said. He couldn't help but join in with the banter. The phone rang to their right.

"It'll be five, maybe ten minutes. Take a seat," Johnny said before scooping the phone up.

Joel turned Livvie and himself around and found a chair for each of them. She looked thankful to be sitting which only made his concern grow.

In five minutes' time, their pizza slices were handed to them and they set upon eating.

He couldn't help but watch Livvie struggle to finish hers, but she needed it more than him, so he didn't offer to help. Wiping their mouths with napkins, they got up and said a quick thanks to Johnny and walked back outside.

It was getting late, Joel guessed it was around eight at night. He started to bike back in the direction of home, toward the hospital, when Livvie asked him what he was doing.

"What do you mean, what am I doing?" he asked.

"Why are you going home?" she said, in a few short breaths.

"Because you said you wanted pizza, but we're going to the hospital now."

"No."

"Yes."

"No. I said pizza then Central Park, Joel."

"That's like an hour away, Livvie," he said exasperated.

"Please, Joel."

He couldn't see her face, but he could imagine it, and that was all he needed to turn the bike around and head toward Central Park.

*

Fifty-seven minutes later, they arrived. Joel got off the bike, but Livvie stayed where she was seated, and he pushed her forward, following her specific directions. They ended up stopping by a field, surrounded by trees. Livvie urged Joel to push them further and further into the middle.

"STOP!" she yelled, giving him a small heart attack. She got off and lay straight down. No hesitation for the wet grass, no nothing.

"Livvie—" he started.

"Joel, just lie down with me, please."

He did what he was told and lay down next to her. Feeling the frost seep through his own clothes, he

*could only hope that Livvie's coat was thick enough
for her to avoid the same discomfort.*

*She moved closer to him, her warmth moving
through him, and she grabbed his hand. She was
looking straight up at the starry sky.*

*"Isn't it beautiful?" she asked him, her voice
shaking.*

"Yes, it is."

*"Ever since I was little, I've wanted to be up there,"
Livvie said.*

*"I know. Usually, a kid wants to be a cat or
something when they grow up, but not you," Joel
said.*

"I know," she answered.

*"One day you might make it up there," he said,
trying not to dismiss her dream of becoming an
astronaut.*

"Maybe sooner than we think…"

"What do you mean?"

*"None of us are going to live forever," she replied
simply.*

*Joel was speechless. How could his baby sister, his
fourteen-year-old sister, think that?*

*"We never know when we will be up there," she
said, unfazed by the concept of death.*

*"Livvie…" His voice caught in his throat. He
swallowed down a huge sob. Didn't she understand
what that would mean?*

*"I love you," she said, looking at him. She had tears
in her eyes.*

Joel loved her with his whole heart. "I love you too, Livvie. Livvie Elaine Lewis, my shining star," he whispered the meaning of her middle name to her. "You're not going anywhere."

She looked away and stared up at the sky again. It was the perfect night to lie under the stars. Livvie squeezed his hand tighter. He didn't know what else to say. He listened to her breaths become shallower and shorter, a gurgling noise filling the air.

He wanted to pick her up and haul ash to the closest hospital, but every time he tried, she fought him. He wanted to pray to God to make her less sick. He wished it was him to get sick instead of her. He wanted to do so much, but he couldn't do a single one of those things. All she wanted was to lie here and look at the stars. He reassured himself that she would be fine, and he would pick her up as soon as she dropped off.

*In the meantime, he instead held her tighter. He instead kissed her on the temple, and he instead whispered, **"I love you"** over and over until she fell asleep.*

She fell asleep. And she never woke up.

Chapter Twenty-Six

Pneumonia fills your lungs with fluid which can thicken into phlegm, clogging your airways. It starves the person of oxygen, making it harder and harder for them to breathe.

I had no idea that was happening to Livvie. No idea she was drowning internally. No idea that she would never wake up again.

The stars took her before I was ready to let her go. It was too fast. Five days ago, I was left completely and utterly alone.

There I was, in front of the station once again, still trying to join her.

I moved into the station, up the stairs and into the main concourse. I felt everything blur together as tears rolled down my cheeks. Guiltiness took over, I never knew she was *that* sick.

Carol, *I'm sorry.*

Livvie, ***I'm sorry.***

My tears were five days too late. I never cried over her dead body. I didn't cry. I didn't feel anything except despair. Livvie was what brought me hope, and I lost that. I lost my one-of-a-kind. I lost my baby sister.

The tears were uncontrollable now, my vision fuzzy. All I could see was the outline of my shoes. I was wishing for the floor to swallow me up, when my shoulder barged into someone else's. I felt myself topple over, my body connecting with the ground. My hands and knees landed on the hard, cold surface. The floor wouldn't be swallowing me up today.

"Dude! What the fork!" yelled the guy who had walked into me.

Automatically I substituted the real swear word for Livvie's made up one. I felt him standing over me and I didn't bother wiping away my tears. I simply turned from my front to my back looking up at him. He wore a clean suit. Well, I assumed it had been clean until he spilled his coffee all over himself. It looked like Gucci too. His face was round, and he looked like he was going to burst from the anger he must have been feeling.

"Hey! I'm talking to you! What are you staring at?" he yelled again, spit spraying in my direction. I brushed my hands off and slowly got to my feet. Tears were probably stained down my cheeks.

"You," I said, unafraid. Any other day, any other moment of my life I would be terrified of him. Not now. Not today.

"Huh?" His anger grew, his face reddening, giving him a new sunburned look. Poor guy. Shrugging I decided not to bother and placed my hands in my pockets, one hand fiddling with the trigger.

"DO you know how much this suit COSTS?!" He stepped forward, getting in my face. This time spit landed on my cheek, drying with my tears.

"Nope," I replied without a care.

"It's a fitted pinstripe Gucci suit. It was three thousand, eight hundred dollars, and now you, idiot, have to buy me a new one."

Was he for real?

"I don't," I replied calmly. I just watched my baby sister die again; I couldn't care less about what I *had* to do.

"What do you mean?!" he yelled.

"I'm not buying you a new suit," I said.

I was definitely not going to buy him a new suit. If he could afford one in the first place, he'd have money for a new one.

"Fork off. Yes, you are," he said, sounding so sure.

"This is what happens when you walk around without a lid on your coffee. Do you want me to spell it out for you? I.T. S.P.I.L.L.S." I said, literally spelling it out for him. This dude was really starting to piss me off.

His face made a funny expression, his lips pulled in a straight line and his eyebrows pointed down as his eyes grew angrier.

Ahhh, fork.

His hand rose, but I was so focused on his face I barely saw it as it slammed down on my cheek, whipping my head to the side and toppling me off balance. I landed back on my butt. *This dude. Really. Just. Slapped. Me?.*

"You, boy, seem like a slow learner. You're paying for a new suit. End of story," he crouched down next to me. People were starting to stare—some entertainment for their morning. *Great.*

"You slap me like my mom does," I said under my breath.

"What the fork did you just say?" His voice grew hot.

I bet I could cook an egg on him from how heated his anger was. The thought made me laugh out loud. His expression changed for a second to confusion. He must have thought I was insane. I didn't blame him.

He grabbed my collar with both of his hands, hoisting me up, back onto my feet.

"Can I cook an egg on you?" I asked, with a slight smirk.

"What?" He was so close I could have kissed him— something I preferred not to do, but it was tempting.

"You're radiating heat cause of how angry you are," I told him.

"What is wrong with you!"

I let him thrust me back to the floor. He stepped over me, legs on either side.

"A lot my dude. A. Lot." I said and welcomed the punch which landed on my nose. I heard a crack, then a scream coming from my left. Then everyone was yelling. The cops will turn up soon, I thought.

Gucci man landed a kick into my stomach, then another to my ribs, and one to my kidney. He pulled me up again by my collar and threw punch after punch until he dropped me. My head hit the ground and blood gurgled up my throat. Its metallic taste made me gag, and I threw it up. *Yip,* he kicked something important.

He stepped away from me. My legs splayed out, but one of my hands still remained in my pocket. I looked up and smiled. This was what I deserved. I could hear Gucci man walking away.

"Hit me again," I yelled after him. "I know you want to…" A mocking tone laced through my voice.

I laughed once I heard his footsteps racing back. He was on me again, hit after hit. It no longer hurt.

He was screaming. I was screaming. Everyone was screaming.

Chapter Twenty-Seven

Tick, tick, tick, echoed through Joel's head. The clock's seconds hand felt like it was inside him. It felt like he had two hearts. Except one was a time bomb counting down. It vibrated through him with every new tick.

Moving his hands, he looked at them, they were babylike. He couldn't reach the floor and his legs swayed unintentionally to the sound of a radio which was coming into focus, playing in the background.

He almost couldn't hear it over the ticking in his head. Was the clock sitting above him? Looking up at the thought, there was nothing except an old, musty panel ceiling above him.

He felt young. Four? Four. He stopped his legs swinging and looked down the hallway. Plastic chairs lined it the walls which was painted a sickly cream that he suspected may have been white once. The floor had a fake-tile look to it. Stains covered everything.

Joel sat in a hospital and a closed door stood in front of him. He wasn't meant to go in there, but he wanted to so badly. Whatever was behind the door was the reason he was there. The silver doorknob looked shiny and it tempted him. All it wanted was to be twisted.

And then it was. It wasn't Joel who twisted it, it was someone coming from the other side. His dad appeared, a smile spread across his face. He gently closed the door behind him, making sure the click wasn't too loud, and then turned to Joel. His eyes were filled with light. Filled with happiness. Filled with love.

"Son, guess what?" Dad's tone was so kind, so soft.

"What?" Joel asked excitedly. The ticking quietened with every new breath.

"You have a new baby sister!" Dad said. Joel was silent for a moment; he had a baby sister. She was born. Excitement filled him.

"Joel? Helloooo? You've been wanting a sibling for ages. Aren't you even the littlest bit excited?" Dad asked. Joel sucked in a breath of air.

"Can I see her?" Joel asked, he sounded calmer than he probably should have been.

"Sure. You ready to be a big brother?" Dad asked again.

"Yes." And he meant it. One hundred percent.

Dad held out his hand, and Joel hopped off the chair. His shoes slapped on the ground. The ticking was gone and Dad's hand was on the knob, twisting it, letting the door push open.

They stood side by side in the doorway. All Joel could see was his mom sitting on the bed—no baby. Her breaths looked labored, she seemed to be hiding something. Discomfort?

It wasn't the glorious sight he had imagined so many times before falling asleep at night. A golden light didn't cast out, blinding him, and then showing him his baby sister. It was dull. It was… it was like a start to a bad ending.

Dad dropped his hand, and Joel just stood there looking at his mom. Her eyes looked pained, filled with sadness. What was wrong with her? Dad walked to her bedside, looking down at something.

"Mom?" Joel's voice came out as a squeak. Mom turned and looked at him. Could she even see him? Was she really there? Why did she look so pale, so out of it?

"Joel, come over here buddy," his dad said. He lifted up something small. It was wrapped almost like a gift. It made a noise. No… she made a noise. She started to cry.

He ran to his dad's side, and Dad kneeled down next to Joel, holding out his little sister.

"You want to hold her?" Dad asked.

Joel nodded eagerly. Dad moved his head to the side, pointing to a chair beside him and Joel jumped on, getting comfortable. He crossed his legs, and Dad slowly lowered her onto him. She was still crying but stopped when she rested gently on Joel's legs. Dad moved one of Joel's hands to under her head,

135

supporting it, he then carefully placed the other on her stomach. Now this is what Joel imagined. She was beautiful. She was an angel already.

"Is Olivia still a good name for her, son?" Dad asked, remembering. He was beaming, radiating happiness. Mom, on the other hand, just looked at Joel, an expression he didn't understand on her face. Joel gave her a small smile, but she turned her head away and stared at the wall.

"Livvie," Joel said, quietly nodding.

Livvie looked up at Joel. Her eyes were so big and round. She had a little bit of hair and her little hand clasped around Joel's finger. She was everything he wished she would be. He already loved her.

"Livvie? Hun, what about that? We can call her Olivia Elaine? Elaine, after your mother? Honey?" Dad asked Mom.

He moved away from Joel, and sat down on the edge of her bed. They talked back and forward quietly. Joel could barely hear them; he was completely focused on Livvie, and she was completely focused on him.

"Joel? Olivia Elaine Lewis... sound good, buddy?"

"Yes!" Joel said

Dad took Mom's hand and gave it a squeeze This time Joel listened in on their conversation.

"In honor of your mother. The amazing Elaine," Dad told her.

"I miss her so much, Tony," Mom said. She sniffled. Her voiced turned to a whisper. "I've carried her for

nine months. Why don't I love her like you two do?"
she asked.

"You will, Honey, you will. You just need time,"
Dad said, trying to soothe her.

"What if I don't?" Mom asked again.

"Don't be silly," Dad told her.

"Mom helped me love Joel. I don't have her now...
How am I going to recover this time? I'm done... she
almost killed me, Tony." Her voice broke off.

"You'll get better, and you have me," Dad said. He
leaned over and gave her a kiss on her forehead.

"Do you want to hold her?" he asked gently. Joel
didn't want Dad to take Livvie from him.

"No, no, let Joel have his time. Why can't I love her
like he already does?" she asked again. She looked
back to Joel. This time he understood her expression.
It was jealousy.

"Well... he didn't have to go through the whole
birthing and pregnancy process so it's a bit easier for
him." Dad chuckled a little, but Mom still didn't look
happy.

Dad gave her another kiss on her forehead. He then
came back to Joel's side, and they both stared at
Livvie. They both had already fallen for their little
shining star.

Chapter Twenty-Eight

He couldn't see. It was dark all around him, and his breathing felt labored, as if an elephant was sitting on his chest.

It was like Joel was trying to suck air through a blocked straw. The pressure started to crawl up his neck, and he felt himself break out into a cold sweat. He lost his balance, falling to his knees. He saw a flash of concrete ground, the same ground he usually restarted on, before his vision turned to black once again.

The concrete was solid, but then it started to stick to him. It moved like a thick liquid, wrapping up and around his knees, pulling him into it. The more Joel moved, the more he sank.

He started to panic. The pressure on his chest felt ten times worse. He couldn't breathe. Joel's heart constricted, the beats becoming quieter with every moment that passed.

The ground was now up to his waist. His arms rested on either side of him, and the thick liquid reached up twisting its way around his arms like a snake. It was almost like oil, the sliminess gripping him, pulling him down, faster.

Joel gave up. Letting it pull him down he stopped struggling to breathe. He just stopped. He felt his upper body fold over, allowing silence to fill him, and the ground sucked him all the way down.

Chapter Twenty-Nine

9:37 a.m.

Inhale, one, two, three.

Exhale, four, five, six.

Inhale, seven, eight, nine.

Exhale, ten, eleven, twelve...

I was breathing? I was breathing. I felt light; I felt free. I was too scared to open my eyes, so I decided to use my other senses first.

Running through them quickly, I figured out that I was still kneeling on some sort of solid ground. I could hear footsteps and people muttering around me. I could also smell rubber... from tires? Or people's shoes?

I knew where I was.

I inched my eyes open slowly, already figuring out that I'd guessed wrong. I was kneeling in the middle of the main concourse under the celestial ceiling, still in Grand Central Station. I didn't start outside this time. I'd restarted already in the place that meant the most to me.

Heat burned through me and I rushed to take my puffer vest off, then I tugged my hoodie off too, completely exposing myself and the explosive vest.

What have I done?

People's voices turned to shouts, and then into screams. I raised my hands to my ears, their echoes cutting through me.

That's when I realized the trigger was on the floor next to me. It lay there like a fallen toy soldier, looking abandoned. I took my hands off my ears and scooped it up quickly.

I finally looked up at the fear I've caused. People ran everywhere. They were like flies, changing direction every minute, smashing into each other.

My ears zoned in on a small boy who was crying, bawling his eyes out. He was all alone, having been separated from his family in the rush I'd caused. I almost walked over to go help him when I heard a father yelling a name over the panicked crowd. He was pushing through a sea of people, yelling "Ethan" over and over.

"Yo, kid," I shouted.

He looked at me. His crystal blue eyes filled with tears, and his bottom lip wobbled.

"Are you Ethan?"

He nodded ever so slightly. His whole body looked like he was going into shock.

"Your dad is right over there, fighting to get to you. How about you help him out and go to him?" I pointed in the direction of his dad. The dad noticed our interaction and seemed to have a surge of adrenaline, pushing through the last of the crowd.

They both raced towards each other, connecting as the dad scooped him up. He eyed me, warily, then made his way back around me toward one of the exits.

I still wanted to die so bad, but I understood now. I felt everything, I was no longer numb. I cared about the people around me now. They had lives. The kid, he was only just starting his, and I didn't want to take that away from him like mine had been taken from me.

I. Don't. Know. What. To. Do.

My breathing sped up, becoming rapid. I started to hyperventilate. I was falling off the edge of another breakdown. I tried to shout, in between breaths, for the remaining people to run, to leave, because I didn't know what I was about to do.

I joined in with the screaming. I couldn't breathe. I couldn't think. *I couldn't... I couldn't do it. I didn't want to do it anymore.*

"Son, I'm going to have to ask you to put that down. Right now," a woman yelled from behind me. I stopped screaming, but I couldn't stop my sobs.

It was much quieter now and I made myself focus on my surroundings. Instead of people's footsteps and screams, I heard police radios going off all around me. I was surrounded.

"Son, please, put the trigger down," the woman said.

She was closer than the others. She was *braver* than the others. Slowly, I turned around, my knees moving carefully on the tiles until I faced her.

She looked tired—she looked stressed, but she was still willing to help. I immediately wanted to hug her. Her dark hair was in a neat bun, her uniform clean and sharp, and she wore a bulletproof vest. She looked about thirty-five. She probably had a family of her own. Her green eyes went nicely with her brown skin. She looked friendly.

"Get away from him, Scarlett," someone called out from behind her, probably another officer concerned for her safety. She took another step closer to me, her arm cautiously reaching out.

"Just place it here, easy as that," she told me, completely ignoring the other officer.

"I don't know what to do," I said in between sobs.

"Help me, help you," Scarlett replied calmly.

"I don't… I don't know. I don't want to hurt anyone anymore." I watched a flicker of curiosity cross her face before she schooled it back into an expression of concern.

"I don't want you to be hurt either," she said, sounding sincere.

"You wouldn't even understand the life I've been through…" I said.

"I can help you." She took another step closer, and someone else yelled out her name.

"Please—"

"Whatever happens, we will get through it together." She took another step.

I could almost touch her hand. "Don't leave me," I whispered.

"I won't, I promise," she told me.

My left hand moved away from my side, and I started to raise it toward her when my wrist twitched. A flash went off behind her. A horrendous boom echoed around us, almost tricking me into thinking I triggered the bomb, until I felt a punch. The weight of a thousand men hit me in the shoulder, throwing me back onto the tiles.

"HOLD FIRE! HOLD FIRE! WHO SHOT THAT ROUND?!" Scarlett screamed, panic lacing her voice.

She ran toward me, falling to her knees. She was crying... Why was she crying?

The yelling around me started up again, but all I could focus on was the blood erupting out of me like a volcano. It was so sick of me that it was racing to leave.

It was like no pain I'd ever felt before. Scarlett went to press down on my wound, and I bit down on my tongue, holding in my scream. I could feel my brain kick into panic mode. She shuffled, releasing a little bit of her pressure and making me release my tongue. I began to gargle blood, spitting it out, spraying it over my own face. Dread gripped me. She turned me onto my side, and it drooled out.

"Wait... wait..." I whispered.

She heard me and leaned her ear down to my mouth.

"I need to get this thing off of me," I said through pained breaths.

Her eyes went wide with shock. She'd completely forgotten about the bomb, but she didn't hesitate. She found the Velcro straps, ripping them open as fast as she could. But she stopped short when I grabbed her hand.

"Let me do it, please…" I whispered, hardly audible. "I need to take it off."

She nodded and helped, pulling me up to a sitting position. The pain was blurring my vision; it was almost unbearable. She let go of me, leaning back out of my way. Her arms hovered around me, like she was ready to catch me if needed. I slowly ripped the rest of the Velcro off, zoning out all the voices in the process.

One handed, I raised the vest over my head, passing my injured arm. The pain in my shoulder almost made me want to vomit. I screamed out and saw a glimpse of stars blurring my vision.

I moved quicker, almost throwing the vest to Scarlett once it was off me. She grabbed it, and our eyes traced down to the wires, connecting it to my injured arm's hand. With the remaining strength I had, I let it slip out.

I slumped back onto the tiles, my arms outstretched. I heard Scarlett rush away, voices now blurred.

I'd freed myself from my own horror, I'd *saved* myself. But as soon as I took the vest off, I couldn't feel her any longer—Livvie. It was like I'd truly lost her presence. My brain had finally come to its senses, finally hearing the emergency alarms going off inside of me. I felt like I'd been injected with what was left of my memories of her, of Livvie, straight into my blood stream and she had vanished from my mind, just like the bomb vest had vanished from my eyesight.

Scarlett rushed back to my side, my shoulder pulsed with pain. She fell to her knees next to me, putting what felt like her whole bodyweight on my wound. My blood heated up with anger. Its escape was now blocked so it found an alternative; blood pooled into my mouth from biting down on my tongue earlier. I started to choke on it silently, letting the blood dribble out. Scarlett wasn't alone anymore as people moved around me.

All the memories, the flashbacks, had put me in agony. They'd made me feel like I was beyond help.

I looked up at the celestial ceiling. *The stars aren't ready for me. I'm so sorry, Livvie.*

I didn't want to die. I didn't want to anymore. I just wanted to see her one more time. I wished she was here, then none of this would have happened. She'd given me so much hope, why should that change? She could still give me hope. I thought I lost it when I lost her, but I'd just been blind to it.

Scarlett grabbed my face, coming back into my view.

"Hey! Hey, kid, stay with me!" Scarlett yelled at me. "We're going to get you through this. You and me, okay?" She held my face with her bloodied hands, blocking out everything else. "Don't you go drifting off. Stay awake!"

She was too late. Maybe the stars were ready. I looked back to the ones on the ceiling which had already started to fade.

Chapter Thirty

Heat shone on Joel's back. Spring was in the air; he could smell it and he could feel it. It was an hour or two before the sun would set. Everything was beautiful.

Joel's hands were curled around his bike's handlebars, and Livvie's blonde hair licked at him in the wind. Joel was ten, and Livvie was six.

Livvie laughed as if her hair was tickling her too. He felt himself smile from ear to ear while biking faster down the road. The whole road was a dream, filled with blossoms.

The wind blew petals around the both of them. They swirled with purpose. It felt like they were lifting Joel and Livvie up. She let go of the handlebars and raised her hands up high. She reached for the petals, trying to catch them as if they were bubbles. Livvie's giggle filled the air. Joel tried to keep the bike stable under her moving weight, having to slow right down.

She let her hands fall back onto Joel's, and he biked off the road, finding a park bench to stop at. Livvie hopped off and sat down on the bench. Joel leaned his bike to the side and sat down next to her.

This was one of their favorite things to do—bike around the streets in the evening. It made them feel free. Free from home, free from school, free from life. It literally brought Livvie alive. And when she was alive, Joel was too.

"Did you see all the flowers?" Livvie asked excitedly.

"Yes, I did." Joel nodded.

"They flew around us." Surprise filled her voice.

"Yes, they did," Joel replied, smiling at her fascination.

They continued talking about whatever Livvie wanted to. She loved to talk, that was for sure. She was a bright light, but throughout the evening Joel felt like he couldn't see her clearly. He rubbed his eyes, only making it worse. His vision completely blurred.

The streetlamp above them had turned on earlier, and he suggested they headed back home. They both hopped back on his bike and rode away.

The wind had died down, and all they could hear was traffic, cars honking their horns, and engines rattling.

Arriving home, they crept in without making a noise and tiptoed to their room, locking their door behind them. Joel jammed a chair under the doorhandle for extra measure.

They both got changed into their pajamas, and Joel helped Livvie get into bed. He went to close the curtain, but she told him to stop. Joel's vision still hadn't cleared. The only thing that wasn't blurry was her eyes. They shone as they stared up into the night sky, stars reflecting in them. He could tell she was smiling without having to see it.

He tucked the comforter up under her chin, and her hands popped out, gripping it. One hand reached up and pressed against the window. His hand gravitated toward hers. He placed his palm over the back of her hand.

"I wish I could touch the stars, Joel. I'm going to be an astronaut one day. I'm going to be up there. I want to be up there," Livvie said eagerly.

"And I'll support you forever and always," Joel replied. He took his hand off hers and gave her a kiss on her forehead.

He went to his bed and climbed in all while focusing on her hand resting against the window. She was now a blur of wonderful color.

"Goodnight, Joel," she said before her hand slipped back under the covers.

"Goodnight, Livvie." The colors glowed, becoming brighter and brighter, blinding him. Joel closed his eyes, giving in to the brightness and opening his ears instead. He heard Livvie's small breaths, her little heartbeat and a siren echoing in the distance. It traveled closer, getting louder with each new second that ticked by as Joel fell asleep.

Chapter Thirty-One

"AHHH!"

A falling sensation took over me.

I bolted upright only to be jerked back. My wrists caught making me hit a soft foam mattress underneath me. I wasn't in front of the station; I wasn't anywhere near it!

A siren wailed above me, and a realization hit me. I was traveling in an ambulance away from the station, and I wasn't dead...

Scarlett and a paramedic scooted back, preparing themselves just in case I lashed out again. They didn't know it was accidental; it was a reflex from my flashback.

"Joel, just relax. The handcuffs are protocol," Scarlett said. She leaned forward just a little, reaching out and touching my hand. Patting it, she tried to communicate with me without any words.

I walked my eyes from her hand on mine to her face, noticing she looked strangely similar to a young Octavia Spencer.

The siren goes off above us again, and I feel the ambulance slow as if navigating traffic.

Why wasn't I in pain anymore? I lifted my head and looked down, an IV needle stuck out of the back of my hand, liquid traveled down to it from a bag above me. It must have been some sort of pain medication, morphine most likely. I hated that I was loving it. I felt so, *so* light.

My shirt had been ripped down the middle. I was so *exposed*. My ribs protruded, and my stomach sunk in the middle. Bile rose in my throat from looking down at myself. Sticky little squares with cords attached dotted my skin—to monitor my heart, I guessed.

Something was wrapped around my right arm, and it tightened slowly. Turning my head to look, I watched the paramedic glanced up from what he was doing.

"Just taking your blood pressure, kid." He pumped the band up to the point where it became uncomfortable. The paramedic looked rough around the edges, like he hadn't slept for the last two nights. He probably hadn't. A hat hid his hair, but he had stubble coming through and wrinkles denting his forehead. He pushed his glasses up from the bridge of his nose. I looked up to his eyes which were a tired blue color. They told me everything.

He read the pressure dial, and I watched him tap it twice on the back of the driver's seat, whispering something to him. The ambulance surged forward in response.

My heart dropped. "Should I be worried?" I croaked out.

"Umm, Joel—" Scarlett began, before choking on her own words. The paramedic took over.

"You've lost a lot of blood from the gunshot wound, and we also think you've suffered from a panic attack of some sorts earlier, which is affecting your blood pressure, so we are just a bit concerned, that's all," he finished. Scarlett nodded a thanks to him.

Earlier, I felt like I couldn't breathe, so a panic attack made sense. I'd kind of thought I was having a heart attack but being only eighteen ruled that out. As well as thinking I was going crazy.

"Thanks," I said, because I didn't know what else to say. Turning my head away, I tried to have a look at where I'd been shot.

The bandage was thick and was taped down over my shoulder. It didn't wrap around, answering another question I had. I didn't have an exit wound.

I'd never imagined that one day, I would have had a bullet stuck in me. *Literally stuck in me.* No doubt I'd end up with lead poisoning or some gnarly infection...

A faint red seeped through to the top of the bandage. It would have had to get through each layer, meaning my blood still wanted to get out of me. Again, I didn't blame it.

A speed bump shook me from my thoughts. Bright lights flashed into the van doors as we reversed back toward the building.

The paramedic got up and started to unplug the monitors attached to me, resting them on my bed. I read his name tag as he leaned over me—John.

Scarlett opened the doors, hopping out and then another paramedic jumped in. His name tag read Angus. Angus looked a bit younger than John. He also wore a hat, and his skin had a nice tan to it. He had dark brown eyes and a dark beard. At least he looked like he had slept last night, *hopefully*.

They finished getting ready and on the count of three, they rolled the bed forward, lifting me out. Flicking the wheels out from underneath the bed, they gently placed the stretcher on the ground.

The ambulance doors thudded shut behind me, and then I was being rolled toward the wide, swinging hospital doors. Scarlett walked right next to me.

I heard the heavy steps they all took, the busyness inside and the wheels rolling over the rough concrete ground. What I didn't hear was my own breathing speeding up.

I hadn't been able to leave the station, but now I have no idea how far away I was from it. Panic gripped at my throat, clogging my airway again. Was I having another attack? Something beeped at my feet—a monitor.

John whipped his head to it before looking down at me.

"JOEL! You need to calm down, right now!" Scarlett basically yelled at me, also noticing my increased heart rate. She tried to seem calm but I could tell she was freaking out. Her face crumbled into one big wrinkle, now full of her own panic. John's glasses wobbled and for a second, and I thought they were going to fall on me when he whipped his head to Scarlett then back to me.

"Get moving, Angus! Run ahead, we will be there any minute. Warn them!" he told Angus, who sprinted ahead to what I assumed was a trauma room.

"Joel? Joel, calm down buddy. It's going to be okay. I want you to try to breathe deeply and slowly through your nose, okay?" John told me. He was the only calm one here. I felt myself nod, but I couldn't get a breath out. My chest was caving in from the immense pressure once again.

They hauled ash toward the trauma room. The wind rushed past me, and it felt like I was flying. Entering the room, about fifteen or so pairs of eyes were trained on me. I was too busy trying to push a breath out of me to count the exact number.

They were all dressed in scrubs, looking clean and just as stressed as Scarlett was. They moved me roughly onto another bed and started hooking me up to all their equipment.

A nurse was at my wrist, trying to get a line in to give me blood. Another filled a syringe with liquid. She went to press it into my shoulder, but I flinched away.

She hesitated. "This is going to help you, bud," she said, looking at me for a second, then pressing it in firmly.

All the chaos around me wasn't helping. The panic grew in my eyes, showing everyone how I was feeling. Doctors barked orders around me, and Scarlett was no longer in the room.

To calm myself down, I tried to zone in on their conversations, something I used to do as a kid when I felt overwhelmed. Closing my eyes, I opened my ears.

"Why'd he close his eyes? Son? Wake up," a doctor asked over me.

"We need to put pressure on his wound; it's still bleeding. It's been what, forty-five minutes now? No exit wound. Get surgery ready," another doctor or nurse yelled.

"The lorazepam injection seems to be working; his heart rate has slowed down," said a nurse. I assumed it was the one who stabbed me in the shoulder with the needle.

"Yeah, it's back down to seventy-two beats per minute," another nurse said.

"Hey, kid, open your eyes. What's his name?" the same doctor asked.

"JOEL!" Scarlett's voice called. She'd made it back in the room.

"Hey, Joel." The doctor rubbed the middle of my chest, my sternum.

Opening my eyes slowly, cautiously, the doctor leaning over me let out a big sigh. "You scared us there. We're going to surgery now. I need to get that bullet out of you ASAP, alright, kid?" he asked.

I was wrong, he must have been a surgeon. He was almost completely bald, probably from stress, but he had a horrific mustache on his face so maybe that's where all his hair went to. He wore thick framed glasses too.

I could feel my breathing slowing down, becoming less rapid.

"We need to get him to sign a consent form, and get his insurance details," another nurse told the surgeon. They handed a clipboard my way and a pen I could only just grip. I signed somewhere on the page, without even a glance at the words. I wanted this bullet out of me.

"You'll be alright, see you soon," Scarlett said, appearing next to me. I watched her walk through the swinging doors, looking down at a walkie talkie in her hand. She turned to another police officer and started talking to him.

I could feel myself being rolled away until I couldn't see them anymore. I put my head back and watched the lights flick past above me. After about two minutes, we rolled into another room. The operating room, I assumed. A different nurse appeared over me.

"Okay, Joel? You ready for a good sleep? Let me just put this over your face." She had curly ginger hair tied in a messy bun and was moving a mask over my mouth and nose. I pulled away from it.

"Get that away from me," I whispered.

"It's to help you go to sleep," she said, again lowering it.

"No," I said.

"No?" Her laser eyes stopped cutting through me as confusion took over her emotions.

"I don't want to restart," I croaked out.

"We need to get the bullet out and stop the bleeding. That'll keep the blood inside you which will help your heart. Now let me put it on," she said in a tone I couldn't disagree with, her laser eyes returning. She put it over my head and turned around to talk to the surgeon.

"He'll be out any minute," she said.

"This wasn't the stress I needed today," he replied.

"Didn't you hear? He was trying to blow himself up," she told him. *Great.*

"How on earth did you figure that out?" Shock traveled through his face.

"Word spreads fast when you're treating a suicide patient," she said.

I decided right then and there, that I didn't like her.

"Well, he's still human, and it's our job to help him," the surgeon said, walking away, probably to the surgery room. She rolled her eyes in his direction and looked down at me. My eyes were hard—they were fierce, and she jumped back in surprise, a hand landing over her own heart as she let out a heavy breath.

"You should make sure your patient is asleep before you talk about them," I said through gritted teeth. The sleeping gas was making me feel groggy as well as grumpy.

I couldn't help it, my muscles untensed, them being forced to relax. My head drooped to the side, my eyes fighting to stay open.

"Goodnight, Joel," Livvie's voice echoed in my mind once more.

I couldn't fight it anymore. I let my eyes close, my breathing becoming more stable. Sleep. Sleep did sound good right now.

Chapter Thirty-Two

"*Livvie?*" I whispered groggily.

Opening my eyes slowly, the white of a hospital ceiling greeted me. I was so cold. Did they have the AC on full blast or something?

This place must not have been able to afford proper bedding because it felt like a sheet of paper lay over me.

Pulling my hand up to scratch an itch on my neck, I fail, once again. Looking down slowly, I found myself still handcuffed. My other hand wasn't, but I was too afraid to move that one. I couldn't even feel it. My whole arm was numb, like it had been disconnected from my brain.

Moving my gaze away from my restrained wrist, I took a slow look around. A curtain surrounded me. No one could see in, and I couldn't see out, but I noticed shoes standing just outside. I almost felt bad for noticing; it felt like I was peeking under a toilet stall. I followed the silhouette up. Whoever it was had big broad shoulders, and they stood like a soldier, unmoving. Was it a guard? Was I being guarded?

I laughed aloud, but it came out sounding more like a croak. I had tried to blow myself up; of course they had someone watching me.

My eyes moved away from the guard, landing on a plastic chair next to me. There was a blur of color, the same colors I saw in my flashback. Was this real?

"Livvie?" I whispered again.

No one replied, but that didn't stop me from talking.

"I think... I think I'm gonna stay alive for a little bit longer, okay? I don't think I'm ready. I think I'll stay here for a little longer, maybe even make you proud, okay?" I finished whispering to the blur of colors, nodding to myself.

I looked away from the chair to find three strangers staring back at me. I mean two. I knew one of them.

It was Scarlett. She was still in her uniform, but her expression seemed sad... worried for me, almost. It had been a long time since someone had been worried about me. I smiled at her which seemed to unfreeze all three of them.

One of the others was a nurse—thankfully not the nurse who put the mask on me earlier. She came forward and straightened the pillow under my head, then checked the monitors beside my bed.

She was petite and had a face full of kindness—kind eyes, kind smile and freckles that sprinkled across her face. Her blonde hair was done in a tight ponytail, and she filled in a checklist, before having a quiet word with Scarlett. It wasn't quite quiet enough, since I still heard her say she was going to get the surgeon to come in and check on me. Scarlett nodded to her and moved forward, followed by a guy in a suit. He held a folder and had glasses hanging around his neck. His hair was slicked back, which made him look a bit sleazy, but who was I to judge?

"Joel, *hi*. How are you feeling?" Scarlett asked. She sat down in the plastic chair.

"Fine and dandy, thanks. How are you?" I asked. The blur of color had gone… unless Scarlett sat on it.

"Great! Good to hear. I'm good, thanks. I'm here to introduce you to your public defender, or can I call you an attorney?" she asked, looking at the man.

He nodded a yes in her direction.

"So, that means he's going to help you with your trial. Is that okay, Joel?" Scarlett asked.

I nodded. Man… a trial. I really hadn't thought this through.

"Okay, well I'm going to leave you two to it, and I'll be right outside if you need anything." As she spoke, she turned in my attorney's direction instead of mine, which I thought was kind of rude. Then again, I did try to blow myself up in a crowded train station…

"The surgeon will come in soon and ask you a few questions, but you don't need to worry about that, okay?" she said, turning back to me.

I said a quiet thanks as she got up to walk out. She didn't completely close the curtains, leaving a little gap, just in case.

In case of what? I asked myself. I couldn't feel one of my arms and the other was handcuffed. I guess I could have tried to kick the guy, but why would I have done that?

My eyes traveled to my attorney—*how fancy*—who sat down in the chair. He started to shuffle through his notes in his lap.

"So, are you gonna introduce yourself, or am I just gonna call you 'Attorney'?" I asked.

He looked up, eyeing me. I could tell he wasn't sure what to make of me. I was just an eighteen-year-old boy who had lost everything and tried to commit suicide—what was there to get?

He lifted his hand for me to shake, but we both looked down at the handcuffs. All I could do was half shrug—half, since one of my shoulders still hadn't regained any feeling.

"Oh, um, yes, okay, sorry. I'm Elijah, your public defender. Unless you have thousands of dollars holed up to pay for your own lawyer, I'm as good as you're gonna get."

I appreciated the honesty. "Hey, Elijah, it's nice to meet you. I'm Joel."

"I know," he said. He didn't need to be so blunt about it. He could have just acted like he didn't know my name.

"Sooo—"

"So, Joel... or would you prefer Mr. Lewis?"

"Just Joel, please."

"Joel. You've made a tricky case for me. Trial is tomorrow. I know. Quick, huh, when there's a potential terrorist sitting in one of our public hospitals." He paused for breath.

"I'm not a terrorist."

"Okay, well that's not what it looks like. Walking into a train station with a bomb strapped to your chest. What were you thinking?" He stopped shuffling through his papers and looked up at me. All I could think about now was how I thought this whole *court* process usually took over a few months to happen, not a few days—*what is happening?*

"I don't know what I was thinking, I—"

"Joel, if you're not honest with me, I can't help you," he said bluntly again.

"I... I wanted to die in the place that meant most to my sister. I wanted to be with my sister. And that was the only place I felt was right..." I admitted, still feeling a little gob smacked about the fact my court day was tomorrow.

"I know you've had a hard life. Your sister died of pneumonia... what? Four days ago? More? Doesn't matter. The police have been looking into your home life. Your mom is messed up, your dad left, you dropped out of school to try and support your sister, before she got sick. It's just been you, alone, trying to pick up the pieces of your life for years. You were bound to break. I don't blame you." He put his glasses on and stared intensely at the paper in his hand. He literally just summarized my whole life, like it wasn't much of a big deal. **My. Whole. Broken. Life.**

"So, what I'm going to try for is a mental disorder defense, a psychotic break, which would also cover the other things you have been charged with. You'll be going to prison either way, but hopefully I can get you placed in a psychiatric wing, or your sentence reduced. If I can't, it'll probably mean you'll get at least fourteen years in prison, most likely a place outside of New York City," he said.

This was going *too* fast. "Fourteen years?" I said, my voice almost broke. *I **really** didn't think this through.*

"But I think if I can get Scarlett to be a witness, she can hopefully express your regret to the judge in the moments before you were shot. Because we both know that you didn't want to hurt anyone else except yourself, isn't that right, Joel?" he asked.

"Yes," I said, almost too quickly. No one except me knew how many times I went through that hell—the number of times I blew people up with me.

"Okay. Good. So, I'm going to keep working on this, and I'll see you later. Don't worry. I think it'll go in our favor. I have a strange feeling about all this," Elijah said. Standing, he ruffled his pieces of papers together before walking out through the gap in the curtain.

As soon as he left, the realization hit me. I was going to go to prison.

"Joel! Buddy! Hey! How are you?" someone shouted at me before moving through the curtain. The surgeon with the massive mustache walked in.

He kept talking, while going around, looking at my vitals, asking for my pain rating and a bunch of other questions which I ignored.

"Hey, Joel?" he clicked his fingers in front of my face, finally snapping me out of my thoughts.

"Yeah?" I said, still trying to come to terms with everything.

"You alright?" he asked. He had a twinge of a British accent. Maybe he grew up in England, but had lived so long in the States, it was now almost non-existent.

He took a seat on the end of my bed, right next to my feet. I bet he never sat on the plastic chairs in the room. Those were for visitors, not him.

I looked up at him. He was staring at me like he cared. He almost looked at me like I could imagine a father would look at one of his kids.

I decided not to lie. "No."

"How come?"

"I just ruined my future, and now I feel like I don't want it anymore." Tears welled up in my eyes. I didn't bother to wipe them away, and the surgeon didn't either. He must have known that I needed to let them out. *I knew* I needed to let them out.

"With that attitude, you won't get anywhere, you hear me? You just need to keep trying. It's all you can do. It's all anyone can do," he told me, with a hundred percent belief in his voice.

"But why can't I do that?" The tears flowed freely now.

"Because you need to have hope. If you have hope, you'll have a purpose," he said.

"And what should I have hope in? This life? It took everything from me." I held down a sob.

"This life took everything from a lot of people. Find the hope in the past. Even if someone special is no longer here, it doesn't mean they still shouldn't give you hope." He looked down at his hands. His eyes glossed over. "You know, I had a son. He was the best boy I could ever ask for. He was filled with so much hope, but one day, life ripped him away from me. I couldn't save him, and I'm trained to save people, to fix people. But I couldn't fix him. Once I finally accepted that, I can now look back on our memories and see the hope he gave me, the hope I felt when I was around him, and there is nothing stopping me from holding onto that." He looked up at me, giving me a smile. A sad but hopeful smile.

"You don't know how much that means to me, sir, hearing that." I sniffled and returned the smile.

"If you have hope… you have everything. There are a lot of broken people in the world, Joel. You're not alone, so just take it easy, yeah?"

"Yes… yes, sir." I felt a little glimpse of hope spark up, defrosting my insides. Already wishing for it to grow throughout my whole body.

Livvie. She would give me hope. *She gave me hope.*

The surgeon stood up to leave. His hand rested on the curtain, ready to open it, but he turned back. "You know, Joel, you were given your name for a reason. It means, The Lord is God. If you can't find your hope, maybe try the Lord's. He's never left me a day of my life." He pointed at the ceiling, I watched his eyes followed his hand upwards before he smiled and closed the curtain behind him.

Chapter Thirty-Three

Elijah, my attorney, came back later in the day to go over a few more things with me. He was curious about my childhood. He sat down in the plastic chair next to me. His suit pants looked strangely oversized. Maybe he had chicken legs.

"So, Joel, can you tell me a bit about your life?" Elijah asked.

"How's that going to help with my case? I thought the police went snooping and told you everything," I replied, bluntly. The pain in my shoulder was becoming stronger. *Give me the painkillers, please.*

"Unfortunately, they couldn't find much. It's almost as if you have been a ghost most of your life. But if I get more background on your life, then maybe the court will take pity on you," he said. He put on his glasses, which had been hanging from a chain around his neck and focused on the papers he was holding.

"I am guilty," I said.

"I know," he agreed. "So help me out with making you look less guilty." This time he looked over his glasses at me with an annoyed expression.

"Fine. How short of a story can I tell you?"

"I just need the facts, Joel." He found a pen in the front pocket of his suit jacket and clicked it on.

So that's what I did; I told him the facts as if I was writing a report. When I thought I was finished, he caught my eye and told me to keep going. He also interrupted whenever he wanted to know more about something I'd said.

It felt so strange telling someone my story. Elijah didn't look up at me. Maybe he wasn't surprised. Was this a daily occurrence for him or something?

"How old were you when your father left?" Elijah asked. Of all things he could have focused on, he asked that?

"Seven."

"Thanks," Elijah said, jotting down my age.

"You're welcome?" I stared at him. I had no idea what he was going to do with all the information I'd told him.

He put down his pen and scooted his chair closer to me. I looked at him, feeling unsure, my eyebrows raised. He stopped when he was right next to me, obviously not scared of me grabbing him or anything—*like I would anyway.*

"Did you hallucinate blowing yourself up, Joel?" Elijah asked, leaning in a little, his voice quieter than before.

"What?"

"Did you halluci—"

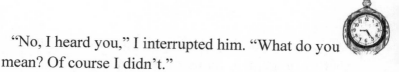

"No, I heard you," I interrupted him. "What do you mean? Of course I didn't."

"The officer with you—what's her name? Argh, it starts with an 'S'. It's on the tip of my tongue..." Elijah's eyebrows furrowed in concentration. I let him be forgetful for another second before helping him out.

"Scarlett."

"Yes!" he said, almost making me jump from his sudden change in tone. "Scarlett. I talked to her while you were in surgery, and she told me that you said you didn't want to hurt anyone anymore? Is that right?" Elijah asked, looking at me intently.

"... Yeah, I did say that," I told him. He almost jumped up with happiness. I was still deeply confused.

"Joel, this is great news," he said.

"It is?" I asked.

"Yes. Can you expand more on why you told Scarlett that?" He clicked his pen back on, ready to write.

"You'll think I'm crazy," I tried to tell him, but he just nodded, waiting for me to continue. *Alright then.*

"I did blow myself up. Multiple times. Each time, I restarted outside the station. Sometimes I wouldn't restart straight away. I'd have these flashbacks... memories. I was reliving my life in little glimpses. Nothing worked. Every time I tried to die, I just restarted..." I trailed off, feeling embarrassed.

171

"You are right, Joel, I do think you're crazy. But that's a good thing for us," Elijah said.

"How?"

"Well…" He ran a hand through his oily, slicked-back hair. The strands didn't move an inch. "No one can restart. It's impossible. I'm not sure what happened to you, but I reviewed the CCTV cameras, and it shows you entering the station only once. You have classic symptoms of someone suffering from PTSD, and I believe you had a psychotic episode." Elijah shuffled the chair back into its usual spot. He gathered his papers together and stood up.

I lay there, a little speechless. He went to walk out through the curtain but then paused, backtracking. Elijah took off his glasses, letting them hang around his neck once again. He came back to the bed and patted my good shoulder with a little smile.

"I'll see you in court tomorrow, bright and early. Oh, and a psychiatrist will be in to see you soon, too," He took his hand away and strolled out through the curtains.

That interaction, that whole conversation was so *strange*. I wasn't sure how to feel about any of it. I was so confused. Man, my head hurts. And now a psychiatrist was coming to confirm whether I was crazy or not…

Chapter Thirty-Four

"Mr. Lewis?" A lady's voice filled the room. She
called out again and then a third time before I decided
to end her suffering.

"Marco?" I called out hoping she would say "polo".
She didn't of course, she did however track down
where my bed was behind the curtain. She pushed it
to the side.

She took a seat and smiled nicely at me. She had
sharp blue eyes, like she would miss nothing. She had
a short blonde bob and pale skin. She almost looked
too young to be a psychiatrist, unless I was
underestimating her age.

"How are you doing, Mr. Lewis?" she asked.

"Amazingly, thanks. You can call me Joel, by the
way."

"Right, okay, Joel. As you probably know—unless
no one told you—I'm a psychiatrist. Your attorney
asked me to come in and assess you. He believes you
may have PTSD," she said almost sounding out of
breath. Maybe she was nervous?

"Cool." I didn't know what else to say.

"Okay, then. I'm going to ask you a bunch of questions which I need you to answer honestly, got it?" she said, finally looking at me. I nodded firmly, earning a tight-lipped smile before she looked back down to her page.

"First one, have you found yourself thinking a lot about troubling events that happened in your life lately? Maybe even having flashbacks?"

I swallowed and nodded. I'd promised to answer honestly, but she was getting straight into it.

"Do you feel that contributed to your actions at the station?"

"Yeah, I wouldn't just decide to blow myself up for no reason, would I?" I asked sarcastically. Hopefully she'd ignore my question.

"Have you been uneasy lately, maybe even jumpy?"

"I've felt pretty numb. Nothing was really putting me on edge except myself…?"

"Have you felt guilty, or unable to stop blaming yourself for what happened?" she asked, but I bet she already knew the answer.

"Of course I blame myself. If I had only noticed Livvie was sick earlier, then maybe she would still be here…" I trailed off. I really didn't want to get into the specifics.

"What about your sleep? How's that been?" she asked, trying to change the subject.

"I haven't really slept for what felt like weeks until they put me under to get the bullet out of me."

"Would you say you felt irritable and angry?"

Wow, what does she think? "Yes." Hopefully a one-word answer would be enough.

"Do you feel you've been able to grieve?"

"I suppose I have in my own way, but I have been avoiding it."

"At any moment, did you feel like what happened wasn't real?" she asked.

"What? My sister dying or me trying to blow myself up?" I asked her.

"Both," she replied quickly and curtly.

"Sister dying felt real but blowing myself up didn't." I knew I should be honest with her and explain about the restarts—the hallucinations, as my lawyer called them. If she wanted to assess my mental state, she needed to know that, but somehow I couldn't make myself tell her.

"How often does your sister come to mind? Or your mom and dad?"

"Almost every time I close my eyes, I see Livvie, but never my dad... occasionally my mom."

"Okay, this is great, thank you, Joel. Just one more question—do you think you're at risk of harming yourself and others again?"

"I'm not sure," I said, watching her write down my last answer. She scribbled some more before she looked up, catching me watching her. "Myself maybe. I don't want to hurt anyone else."

"Alright, thanks, Joel. That about does it for me. Hope you feel better soon," she said before hopping up and leaving.

175

She didn't really seem like a psychiatrist, but I guess she'd made her assessment. She'd come to a conclusion about whether I had PTSD by looking at what the others had gathered too. I wasn't sure how I felt about this whole thing. Mostly overwhelmed.

I laughed a little out loud, almost as if I was nervous and it had been a delayed response to the psychiatrist coming in. I rested my head back on the pillow, letting my eyes close slowly. All this talking about feelings was strange to me. I wasn't used to it in the slightest…

*

The rest of the day was filled with nurses waking me up and visits from the occasional cop, which involved poking their head through the curtain checking if I was still there.

They didn't need to worry; I wasn't going anywhere. Even if I wanted to, physically I couldn't, unless I learned how to pick locks or how to dislocate my thumb.

The pain in my shoulder came in pulses, and the nurses told me that they were having to drop the pain medication, since I'd be out by tomorrow morning. They didn't want me addicted to the stuff. That was fine by me. I did not want to be addicted to anything. I would not become a monster like my mom. *So pain, come at me.*

Chapter Thirty-Five

I woke up the next morning, slightly surprised to be staring up at the hospital ceiling instead of a massive concrete building. My head felt all muddled up. It would take me a while to get used to this.

The curtain was pushed to the side by two nurses dressed in scrubs and the sun rushed through a nearby window, striking me in the face.

At first, I felt shock, dread, and fear, but then I focused on the sun. It felt similar to when I'd ridden to Grand Central Station. The light barely reached me, but somehow, it still filled me with warmth and hope as the two nurses worked around me.

One nurse took out my IV and the other positioned my arm into a sling. They helped me into a pair of sweats and a hoodie that they must have found in their lost property bin. The clothes were massive on me, and one of the nurses had to roll up the sweats. I looked pretty funny, since I only had one arm through the sleeve. The other sleeve flopped to my side, lifeless. At least the top and bottom matched—gray on gray. The nurses helped me slip on my old shoes and tied my laces.

I felt completely useless, like a little child, but I thanked them anyway once they were finished. They both gave me polite nods but were too scared to look me in the eye. The officer who stood guard outside my curtain then came in and put me in a wheelchair, pushing me down several corridors and into the elevator before we reached the front doors of the hospital.

A police car was barely visible as countless reporters stood eagerly waiting for my arrival. You would have thought I was famous or something. Well, I suppose technically I was. I had tried to blow myself up in one of the most public places in New York.

Standing up, out of my wheel chair, we walked through the doors and microphones, cameras, and questions were thrown at me like grenades. The reporters bumped into me, trying to get as close as they could. One bounced into my shoulder, and I let out a yelp.

The officer kindly put up my hoodie and pushed me forward through the crowd. He barked at the people to move away, to give me space, but no one was listening.

I'd never felt claustrophobic before that moment, but now it felt like everything was closing in. Finally, we reached the side of the police car, I opened the door myself. I had to get out of there; I could feel another panic attack coming on, and I did not want to break down in front of all the cameras.

I jumped into the back seat, yelping again as my arm jolted. The officer didn't join me. He shut the door and tapped the roof twice, indicating for the officer at the wheel to take off. I turned around and watched through the back window as the cop was swarmed with people. All I could see was his hand up in the air before we turned around a corner.

I chose to zone out as we drove toward the courthouse. Other cars passed by, blurring into colors.

We didn't pull up to the front entry of the courthouse, once we saw the reporters positioned outside. They drove around the back of the building instead. One of the officers opened the car door for me, and I scooted out. The other took hold of my good arm. He was dressed in his uniform, wearing his hat and everything. He was clean-shaven, and he avoided eye contact with me, looking ahead to the other officer walking out in front.

This officer was also wearing his uniform and his hat, but he had a slight limp which made him drop his right side down with every new step. *I think I'll name these two "Eyes" and "Limpy".*

I read the sign as we passed through the back entrance: "Welcome to New York County Criminal Court".

We walked down a series of corridors, lit by artificial lighting, not a window in sight. The walls were cold concrete blocks making it feel like I was already in prison.

A few turns later, we pushed through double doors, entering a courtroom. Everyone was already there, except me and the judge. I felt like I should have apologized, but I couldn't bring myself to say "sorry" out loud.

At least this room had a few windows. Aside from that, it was very plain. Dark oak wood and creamy yellow walls weren't a good mix.

As *Eyes* and *Limpy* walked me down the aisle, I recognized six people sitting in the row behind my attorney. Scarlett, the surgeon, the psychiatrist, the little boy who got lost at the station and his parents, and lastly, Dufty. Seeing Dufty made my heart hurt.

Officer *Eyes,* who was holding my arm, sat me down in a chair next to Elijah and handcuffed me to the armrest. Elijah was dressed in a suit that actually fitted him. His glasses were already on the bridge of his nose, his hair was still slicked back, this time so tight that it pulled at his face. He gave me a hope-filled smile, but I couldn't stop thinking about why Dufty was there. I looked back to him, and his eyes found mine. Tears brimmed on his lashes as he gave me a sad smile.

Dufty brought back memories that I didn't want to think about, but not all of them were bad...

Joel rushed through Dufty's coffee bar door with his bike and Livvie after a day at school. Mud caked his

*wheels. As he pushed the bike through the dining
area, dirt dropped onto the floor. Everyone stared at
Joel, and he put his head down, following Livvie into
the back.*

*He left his bike in front of the dishwashing sink and
got Livvie settled in the chair Dufty had left for her.
Joel took off his hoodie, making a cushion for her
bottom. It was going to be a long night. She got a
book out of her school bag and went into her own
little world.*

*He loved watching her read. Her mouth would
move, sounding out the words, and her eyebrows
seemed to point into a frown when she concentrated.
She was beautiful.*

*"JOEL!" Dufty yelled through the kitchen doors.
Joel stood up straight immediately and walked out to
the front.*

*"Yes, sir?" Joel looked down to the marks his bike
left all over the floor. His heart dropped into his gut.*

*"What is this on the floor?" Dufty said pointing at
the mud.*

*"Tracks from my bike, sir. Sorry, it's been raining a
lot and I didn't want to be late for work." Sheepishly,
Joel looked down, ashamed.*

"Joel?" Dufty asked.

"Sir?" Joel kept his head stiff, focusing on the floor.

*"Look at me, Joel," Dufty spoke calmly. Joel looked
up slowly and made eye contact with him. "Being late
won't make me pay you any less. Next time pick the
cleaner, safer way to come to work. I would hate to*

*hear you and Livvie got into a bike accident. Okay,
son?"*

*"Yes, sir," Joel replied. His heart jumped back up
to where it belonged. He went to turn around when
Dufty placed his hand on his shoulder.*

*"You don't need to be scared of me. You're the best
dishwasher boy I've ever hired. I'm not going to fire
you over something this silly. I don't think I'll ever
fire you, Joel." Dufty looked at him closely and then
brought him into a hug. Joel didn't know what to do
with himself. He hadn't been hugged in so long; he'd
forgotten what it felt like.*

*"How about we get a mop and bucket and clean this
up?" Dufty spoke softly. Joel nodded into his chest,
still enclosed in the hug.*

*Dufty released him, then reached over to his cabinet
and broke a soft pretzel in half. He handed one part
to Joel. Dufty knew that Joel would have given the
whole thing to Livvie, if given the choice. Dufty then
walked into the kitchen with the other half, giving it to
Livvie.*

*Joel watched them interact for a minute. Livvie
loved Dufty, and he was so good with her. Dufty
grabbed the mop and bucket, filled it up with hot
soapy water, and brought it out to the front.*

*"Dufty, I can do that. I'll mop," Joel said, already
feeling bad for making more work for him.*

*"Don't be silly, you have a pretzel to eat," Dufty
told him and started to clean.*

Chapter Thirty-Six

"All rise!" shouted the bailiff to my side, bringing me back to reality. I shook my head to refocus when I noticed a deepening ache at the base of my skull— *maybe I hit my head when I got shot?*

I stood out of habit, but my hand tugged me back. I completely forgot that I was handcuffed. My chair tipped, jerking off the floor with me. I heard someone let out a chuckle behind me, my clumsiness amusing them.

I wasn't sure if I was supposed to stand or not. I'd never been to court before. I looked back to Elijah who shook his head in embarrassment and covered a smile with his hand.

The bailiff gave me a look of "I can't believe you just did that" before continuing to speak. "Court is now in session," he said. "Judge Philips presiding. Please be seated."

Everyone around me took their seats. I tried to, but my chair had a mind of its own, and trying to reposition it with one arm was a struggle.

Elijah came to my aid before I made a complete fool of myself, and then returned to his own seat.

The judge watched me with fierce eyes. Her blonde hair was pulled back into a tight bun, and her judge's robes seemed three times too big for her. She also seemed to be struggling to make herself feel comfortable at her bench. Still looking at me, she began to speak.

"Good morning, ladies and gentlemen. Calling the case of Mr. Lewis forward. Are you ready?" she aimed the question toward Elijah who nodded confidently.

"Will the clerk please swear in the jury?" she asked the lady below her who nodded and stood, walking toward the jury. The jury contained twelve people. Twelve people I had never seen before in my life. The court was putting my life in the hands of strangers. *Better than no one*.

"Will the jury please stand and raise your right hands?"

The jury did as they were told.

"Do each of you swear that you will fairly try the case before the court, and that you will return a true verdict according to the evidence and the instructions of the court, so help you, God? Please say I do."

They all did, and the clerk told them to be seated. She took a seat herself.

There was a minute of silence before Elijah stood up, shuffling his pages. He walked forward to talk to the jury.

"Your Honor, ladies, gentlemen of the jury; the defendant has been charged with attempting acts of terrorism, attempted murder, attempt to cause grievous bodily harm, and attempt to destroy public property. Even if Mr. Lewis had the intent to cause the evacuation of the Grand Central Station, I don't believe he was mentally aware of what he was doing. All his attempting only caused himself harm."

I was surprised by the confidence in his voice, but also by how guilty he was making me look.

"According to the National Child Traumatic Stress Network, trauma occurs when a child experiences an intense event that threatens or causes harm to his or her emotional and physical well-being, which started happening to Mr. Lewis before the age of seven. This can result in lasting mental and physical effects such as long-term psychiatric and behavioral difficulties including criminality, as my defendant has portrayed." Elijah took another breath, and the judge cut him off.

"Get to the point, attorney," she told him.

He turned pale for a second and glanced back at me, clearing his throat before continuing.

"Trauma like this means that Mr. Lewis may suffer from flashbacks, nightmares, hallucinations, which he has confirmed with me. He told me that he had blown himself up numerous times and had seen his deceased sister on many occasions while trying to commit suicide. Mr. Lewis has experienced the three E's, events, experience, and effects. This left Mr. Lewis believing that it was perfectly fine to try to commit suicide in the way he did. From the medical assessment I have given everyone, you'll see Mr. Lewis is suffering from Post-Traumatic Stress Disorder and depression. On the day in question, Mr. Lewis was experiencing a psychotic break, stemming from his PTSD and resulting sleep deprivation. He was not in his right mind, and therefore cannot be held responsible for his actions. I strongly urge you to take this into consideration, and find him not guilty by reason of insanity," Elijah finished strongly and took a step back.

"Would you like to call any witnesses?" Judge Philips asked Elijah.

"Yes, your Honor. Doctor Ava Owens, please come forward."

Ava, who was my psychiatrist, stood and moved out of the row before briskly making her way up to the witness stand. Her heels had clicked with every step down the aisle. Once she stopped walking the click continued to echo in my mind.

The clerk met her at the podium. "Please stand. Raise your right hand. Do you promise that the testimony you shall give in this case before the court shall be the truth, the whole truth, nothing but the truth, so help you God?"

"I do," Ava said.

"Please state your first and last name," the clerk asked.

"Ava Owens."

"You may be seated," the clerk said, and walked back to her own seat.

Elijah then walked forward from where he was waiting, and started with his questions.

"Doctor Owens, I understand you saw my client here during his stay at the hospital? Is that right?" Elijah asked.

"Yes."

"What were you doing there?"

"I was asked to see Mr. Lewis to assess his mental state," she answered.

"So, you're a psychiatrist?" Elijah asked. I thought it was a dumb question, but I guess the jury wouldn't know.

"Yes, I have been for six years now."

"What type of assessment did you do on my client?"

"I asked him questions that helped me understand how he was doing—mentally, I'm meaning. Mostly questions to do with PTSD."

"What was your conclusion, Doctor Owens?"

"From the answers I received, I do think Mr. Lewis is suffering from PTSD and has been for a long time." she said. I'm not sure how she came to that result, I didn't really tell her much at all. Maybe it was my *tone?*

"If my client has been suffering from PTSD, let's say for more than a year… do you think that could have caused him to have a psychotic break from a recent event which just pushed him too far?"

"Yes, I think that could have been the case."

"That's all. Thank you, Doctor Owens," Elijah said, dismissing her like he was a teacher.

Ava stepped down from the stand, giving a tight smile toward Elijah before making her way back to her row, sitting down beside the surgeon. The click of her heels came back and the ache at the base of my skull had now travelled up, stabbing me behind my eyes.

Honestly, I thought that whole conversation was kind of rude...

"The next witness I would like to call forward is Constable Scarlett Daniels. Please could you come forward?" Elijah called out.

Scarlett stood and made her way forward. The bailiff took her to the witness stand.

The clerk met her there and repeated the whole swearing-in process again.

Elijah walked toward Scarlett and asked her what she did for a job—a silly question really since she was still in her uniform, but she answered it anyway. The next question was more suitable, as he asked her about the events that happened three days ago.

"Well, to put it frankly, I got called in for a potential bomb threat in the station and when I got there, Joel here, he was kneeling with his fists against his head, crying out for someone called Livvie. As I got closer to him, he started to calm down. He really didn't want to hurt anyone. When he was passing me the trigger, I think his hand flinched making an officer fire a shot, hitting him in the shoulder." She gave me a soft smile before looking back at Elijah.

"Did he still give you the trigger?" Elijah asked.

"Yes, he did," Scarlett confirmed.

"And was he planning on doing what you had asked before he got shot?"

"Yes, and he took off the bomb voluntarily too. He told me he wanted it off."

"Thank you, Miss Daniels. One last question—do you believe he wanted to hurt anyone?" Elijah asked.

"No," Scarlett replied.

"Thank you, I have no further questions." Elijah stepped to the side. The judge dismissed Scarlett, and Elijah called up the next witness, the little boy. The boy was wearing his best dress shirt with some long khaki-colored pants. The clerk went through the whole process with him, and he looked genuinely terrified. Elijah stepped forward.

"Hey, buddy. You okay?"

"Yeah." His voice came out like a timid little mouse. His cheeks were red as if he had been crying before the session had even started.

"Don't worry, you're not in trouble. This won't take long," Elijah said, trying to comfort him. "Did this man over here," Elijah pointed at me, "help you?"

"Kind of," the kid told him.

"Okay, how did he kind of help you?"

"He told me where my dad was," he squeaked out.

"That was nice of him, and did you think he was going to hurt you?"

"…No, I don't think so." The kid looked over to me, unsure.

"Okay, I have no further questions." Elijah smiled and helped the kid get down from the witness stand. "I have one more witness to call, your honor."

"Go ahead," Judge Philips said.

"Could Dante Ricci come to the front, please," Elijah asked.

I watched Dufty stand… I never knew that his real name was Dante.

He was wearing his best suit, and the little hair he had left was combed over. His brown eyes were filled with worry. Dufty made his way to the witness stand slowly without taking his eyes off me the whole time. He promised to tell the whole truth and nothing but the truth, and then stated his first and last name.

"How do you know Mr. Lewis?" Elijah asked him.

"He walked into my shop one day with his little sister, and asked for work. I think he was fourteen at the time," Dufty said. He hadn't forgotten.

"How long did he work for you?"

"Oh, a long time. Four years, I think. He stopped turning up about seven maybe eight days ago. It broke my heart, but I hoped he'd come back," Dufty said smiling toward me.

"Why do you think he stopped?" Elijah asked.

"I think the place reminded him of his baby sister too much. They spent a lot of time there. She— Livvie, Joel's sister—died, but I didn't find out until a few days ago. I had no idea she had gotten so sick," Dufty told the jury.

"From what you knew of Mr. Lewis, did he have a stable home?" Elijah asked.

"No. He used to work night shifts, but I would always send him home just after midnight so he would get sleep for school the next day," Dufty said.

"So, he used to work night shifts to avoid going home, is that what you're saying?"

"I suppose I am, yes."

"Did he ever talk about home?"

"No, but Livvie did," Dufty said, looking at me. Tears started to stream down his face. "I wish I'd done something, you know? I wish I could have gotten you help. But the only thing I did was pay you more than you should have earned. I thought you were just being a good boy by helping your parents out, but it was so much worse. I am so, so, sorry Joel. I am so sorry—"

"Thanks, that's enough now. No more questions," Elijah said, cutting Dufty off. The bailiff helped Dufty step down and guided him back to his seat. The whole way back, Dufty kept saying sorry. I tried to count, but it was impossible.

"Would your defendant like to testify, Attorney?" Judge Philips asked Elijah. He looked at me and I nodded. The officer undid my handcuffs and brought me up to the witness booth. I then also promised to tell the whole truth to anything they asked of me. The lightning was different from this angle, it was sharper.

"Mr. Lewis, what was your plan for October twenty-third," Elijah asked, almost seeming hesitant of my answer. I almost winced when I looked toward him, the sudden movement made me feel like the inside of my head was an ocean in the middle of a storm, my brain hitting the sides.

"I planned to die, sir. I wanted to die in my sister's favorite place. I wanted to die," I told him ignoring the pain. I told the jury. I told the judge. *I told* Dufty.

"Did you want to hurt anyone?" Elijah asked.

"No one, but myself." *Not at first, anyway.*

"So, you planned to tell everyone to leave, before you detonated your explosive?"

"Yes, most people figured it out once they saw the trigger, so it never took very long for everyone to run away from me," I said.

"No more questions, your Honor," Elijah said as he walked back to his seat. I followed him back to mine, and the officer again handcuffed me to the chair. Admitting that had exhausted me.

Elijah gave the judge a curt nod toward before he sat down, joining me. As soon as he did, his calm exterior broke and his knee started to bounce.

"The prosecution may begin their case against the defendant," Judge Philips said, moving her attention to the lawyer sitting on the other side of the room. I hadn't even noticed him until a second ago. He strode to the front of the room, looking smug. He knew he was going to win without even trying.

He wore a clean beige suit. His hair was brown, and he had that kind of face that could annoy you just by looking at him.

"Your Honor, ladies and gentlemen of the jury, hello, how are we all doing today? Good? Good. The defendant here," he said, spinning my way with an accusing hand before continuing, "has been charged with the acts of terrorism. Did we hear that correctly? Let me repeat. Terrorism. He has also been charged with attempted murder, attempt to cause grievous bodily harm, and attempt to destroy public property. I know, I know, none of these things happened but imagine if they had—he would be on death row already. And that doesn't mean he still shouldn't be..." He paused letting it all sink in.

I could feel my heartbeat speeding up. Death row? I didn't think we had the death penalty in New York, maybe that's changed. I felt like I was going to black out.

"Mr. Lewis here thought of how he wanted to go out. Honestly, kid, it could have been easier to jump off a bridge than choose one of the most crowded places to go out in—"

"Your Honor, objection, conjecture," Elijah said, jumping up, giving me a fright.

"Objection sustained. State facts, Bailey. First and final warning," the judge said. Huh, so that's the ash's name, Bailey, it was probably his last name though.

"Yes, I apologize. Continuing on with my case, I would like to recall Officer Scarlett Daniels," Bailey said.

Scarlett started to shuffle her way toward the stand again when I heard the back door open. Looking down the aisle, completely distracted from my case happening in front of me, I saw *Carol...?*

Chapter Thirty-Seven

She shuffled slowly but surely toward Joel, but she definitely took her time. He couldn't believe she was here. How did she know where to come? How did she know... Wait. Joel frowned. She couldn't remember him; she'd never met him... unless she had? Was it possible the restarts left some memories behind for the people he had met during them?

Joel couldn't believe what he was seeing. He rubbed his eyes with his one good arm and blinked again. She wore the same thing he'd seen her in last—a gold watch, pearl jewelry, a plain cardigan that wrapped around her shoulders, black trousers, and lastly, her hair was styled the same way as it was before...

No, this couldn't be real...

She reached Joel and took a seat right beside him. Was she allowed to do that?

"Hey, boy, how you doing?" she asked in the same blunt tone as their last conversation. He found a sense of familiarity in it, even if it did shock him.

Joel just stared at her. If he stared at her hard enough, maybe this would all disappear... but nothing changed. Carol sat patiently beside him waiting for his answer.

"Uh, you can see how it's going, can't you?" he asked, making a small gesture around the room. As he did, he also looked around. Everyone seemed to be frozen or perhaps moving at the slowest pace possible. His brain couldn't wrap around what was happening to him. Was he about to restart?

"Well, you did want to go out with a bang, didn't you?" Carol asked him, bringing his attention back to her. He recalled in their last conversation how she wanted to leave with him, and that she'd told him to run if he had any feelings of regret. He had stayed put, but he didn't want to.

"I'm sorry," Joel apologized.

"What for?" Carol asked, now looking a little puzzled. One of her hands moved to his, resting on it gently.

"I didn't want to die. You told me to leave if I felt even a hint of regret, but I stayed for you. I did it, that time, for you."

"Well, that was silly of you," she said, almost dismissing the matter like he was a child.

"I lied."

"People lie. Often. I just wish you hadn't. Maybe you wouldn't be in this mess if you'd left me then." She looked at him sternly. Maybe she couldn't look away…?

"I can't believe you remember what happened," Joel said, finally letting a big breath out. No one else understood.

"Strange isn't it... what do you think it all means?" she asked.

"What do you mean?"

"All of this, this mess you've created," she said, gesturing around.

"I'm not sure..." he said, reflecting on her question.

"Are you going to be alright, boy?" Carol asked him.

"Maybe... time will tell," he said, watching her reaction. Almost nothing changed in her face. Their last conversation was basically all about time and the life she lived, but maybe she didn't really remember? No. No. No! This couldn't be real! He couldn't restart now!

He looked around in a panic. He even stood up with ease, his arm gliding right through the handcuff still hooked to his chair. Fork.

"Joel?" She moved her head slowly, she looked up him, making Joel feel extremely uncomfortable at the angle of her head. This wasn't real. Please let this be a dream. Please.

"Don't worry about me, I'll be fine. Heck, I'm not even real, but I hope you have a great life after all this drama gets sorted," she said, so normally.

"What...?" Has Carol always been a figment of his imagination?

"You're in more control than you realize; all the best," she said, another cryptic message for him to mull over. She moved to stand up. Her movements were no longer swift but rigid, almost robotic even. He reached out to help, sliding his hand under hers, but all he did was glide through her.

"What is going on? Carol? Are you even here? What the actual fork!" Joel yelled in any direction. He went to help her again, so sure she was actually there. He held out his arm for her to hook hers in, when he felt a pulling sensation. Finally, something real. She must actually be here.

Except, when he looked down to where her hand would have been, he saw nothing. Complete and utter darkness consumed his surroundings. This couldn't be happening again, why again?

Joel stamped his foot in frustration, but when it made impact with the ground he went into a free fall. He just fell. Wind whooshed past him. He reached out to grab anything, but there was nothing. He kept falling, neither knowing how long he'd been falling for nor when it would end.

It was all **nothing.**

Chapter Thirty-Eight

"Joel? Mr. Lewis? You need to snap out of it. Joel!" Elijah yelled at me.

My eyes flinched then opened, I didn't restart... I scanned everyone's faces. They were giving me the strangest looks.

"Elijah, what happened?" I said, surprised at my own voice. It was croaky, like I'd been asleep for twelve hours. My whole body felt surprisingly relaxed, and the pounding pain in my head and shoulder had stilled. But I could feel it begin to rise back up.

"Bailey started his side of the case, and you just slumped over. None of us noticed until you started flinching around like a dead fish. You blacked out..." He stared at me, concerned.

"Oh."

"Oh?" he said, before Judge Philips interrupted him.

"Is your client fine to go on, Elijah?" she asked.

"I am not sure, your Honor..." he said, breaking eye contact with me.

I moved, resting my back against my chair. I blacked out. I didn't restart.

"People of the jury, it's time for you to deliberate. Attorney, please make sure your client is well enough to hear the outcome when we reconvene," Judge Philips said, standing, she stepped down from her bench and walked out a door behind her. The jury followed after her. Bailey must have finished his side to the case before they noticed me unconscious, which I was secretly thankful for.

I didn't know what to do or say; I was speechless. This all felt like a movie.

*

Exactly thirty minutes later, we were called back into the courtroom, and the judge and jury walked back in. We all stood and then sat down again once they were seated. The judge cut straight to the point and asked the jury foreperson whether they had reached a verdict, which they said they had. They passed their conclusion over to the clerk who stood.

"On the charges of domestic terrorism and attempted murder, the jury finds the defendant, Joel Lewis, not guilty. On the charges of attempt to cause grievous bodily harm, and attempt to destroy public property, we find the defendant guilty," she said, and sat again. She started to shuffle her papers together as if she was about to leave.

What did that mean? I turned my head slowly to look at Elijah, but he was staring at the judge.

"Mr. Lewis, you will be detained at Blakewater Correctional Facility to await sentencing. The jury is thanked and excused. Court is adjourned." With that, Judge Philips hit her hammer down and swiftly left.

Before I even knew what was happening, I was being moved out of my seat and back out of the court's doors, down the many corridors, and to the back entrance.

"We did it, Joel! This is a really good outcome, considering the circumstances. I reckon you'll be out in seven years or so," yelled Elijah from behind me.

I was going to prison, so it still didn't feel like a win for me, but it was better than fourteen years for terrorism.

"I'll visit once a month, got that?" Dufty's voice echoed out behind me. "I'll see you soon, son. I'm so sorry."

I wanted to turn around and give him a hug, but the officer holding my good arm was too strong. If Dufty kept his promise, then I would tell him that I had forgiven him. It was never his fault to begin with.

I smiled to myself. At least I didn't have to worry about paying for food or a place to sleep for the next seven or so years. It would be good for me to have some routine again. To be stable for a while.

Officer *Limpy* was out in front, opening the back doors of the building, the same entry we'd come in through. Security held back reporters on either side of the steps, and a van waited with its doors open.

The sky was a dull gray color; rain was probably on the horizon.

The reporters were smart enough to come around to the back of the building, and they hurled question after question in my direction. A few members of the public were there too, but instead of questions, they threw abuse. *Nothing I wasn't used to.*

I looked down at my feet again and made it to the van, hopping in. Officers *Eyes* and *Limpy* slid in next to me and closed the doors behind them.

I was going to prison. ***Right. Now.***

Chapter Thirty-Nine

The van came to a stop, jolting me forward. My handcuffs and the chain anchoring me to the floor pulled me back into my seat. The stop broke me out of my daydream, or was it a daymare? I was going to prison. Actually, I was already there, and I was about to walk through its doors. My nerves were eating me away.

The van doors swung open. Officer *Eyes* unlocked the chain from my handcuffs and motioned for me to follow Officer *Limpy*, who was already out of the van.

I stepped out, looking up, only to be blinded by lights. Bright fluorescent bulbs flashed at me like they were having a seizure. My head felt close to exploding. I raised my arm to cover my eyes, waiting for my pupils to adjust.

Officer *Eyes* grabbed me by my shoulder, pushing me forward. Only then could I feel the people around me. I felt the thudding of everyone's footsteps. I felt their presence before I could see them; before I let myself hear them.

The noise hit then me, smashing into me like a boulder. People were shouting my name, and nicknames I assumed were also *mine.*

"KILLER!"

"MONSTER!"

"JOEL! LOOK OVER HERE FOR US, BUDDY!"

"DIE IN HELL!"

The abuse kept coming.

My arm still covered my face as I continued to move forward. I was thankful for Officer *Eyes* behind me for helping with that. I didn't know what I would've done if I'd had to walk alone through that crowd. I probably would have sat on the ground and cried myself into a puddle.

Finally, a slam echoed behind me, shutting the crowd outside. Their volume dropped to a low mumble.

I allowed my arm to drop as I sighed, letting out a huge breath. A simple wooden counter holding a few computer monitors stood in front of me, and some plastic chairs were to my right. *It looked like a waiting room for visitors...?* The walls were a sickly yellow, making it oh so inviting, and let's not even begin on the floor.

Officer *Eyes* pushed me forward again, up to the counter. A lady with her hair held up in a clip looked over her glasses. She had a pointed nose and a pointed chin too, probably because her face was pulled so tight. Her lips were plump, covered in a sticky lip gloss, and eyelash extensions added to her fakeness. She batted them our way.

"Hi, darlin', sign your life away. Put all your personal belongings in here and welcome to hell," she said, without a hint of glee. Her voice reminded me of Janice off the show *Friends*—whiney and annoying, and I'm glad she didn't attempt to laugh.

She thrust forward a container that already had my name on it. I took the pen and signed my name away. This—the mess I'd made—meant the consequences were inevitable.

I took the container, and Officer *Eyes* laid his hand on my shoulder again, guiding me forward to another door. Officer *Limpy* opened it, and we all entered. I heard the click of it locking behind us. There was another door, leading to what I guessed were the cells.

I put the container on the bench beside me and noticed a bright orange jumpsuit, white sneakers, white socks, a tank top and black boxer briefs. This was going to be awkward.

"Strip," Officer *Limpy* said while taking my handcuffs off.

"Excuse me?" I answered back, almost lost for words.

"You heard him, kid. Take off your damn clothes and put them in the container with everything else you have on you, including the sling," said Officer *Eyes*. They both sounded like they wanted to be anywhere else but here.

"You could have asked me on a date first or something, *gosh*." I already regretted saying it halfway through speaking as *Limpy* and *Eyes* pushed me up against a wall, their faces inches from mine. My shoulder instantly felt like it was on fire.

"My daughter goes through the station every day to get to work," Officer *Eyes* told me.

"You better watch it, kid, or we will have to do a thorough search on you, and it won't be pretty," Officer *Limpy* spat into my face.

"Okay, okay, fine. I'm sorry."

They put me down and stepped back, like it was normal to threaten everyone who came into here. I turned around and started taking off my clothes awkwardly, one-handed.

"Facing us," Officer *Limpy* barked.

I looked at them, disgust written all over my face, as I turned myself toward them. As quickly as I could, gritting my teeth from the pain, I took everything off and dropped it into the container. I covered my privates and reached for the new clothes when they stopped me again.

"Do a twirl for us," Officer *Eyes* said.

"What?"

"Twirl."

I didn't risk being told again and did a full three-sixty before grabbing the new boxers and sliding them on. I put everything else on and sat down to tie up my shoes. That's when I made another mistake. I should never have sat down.

A knee came into my eye line, driving straight into my face. My head whipped up, blood already rushing down my nose. I barely had any time to react when a fist slammed into me, knocking me sideways and causing me to fall off the bench. I caught myself on my hands and knees, my shoulder screaming, then a kick landed into my gut. Instinctively, I crawled into a little ball and waited for the abuse to be over.

After a few minutes, Officers *Limpy* and *Eyes* sounded out of breath. They reached down and hauled me up by my arms, handcuffing me again. I could barely stand. The pain I felt earlier in my shoulder transferred to my entire body. Everywhere ached.

My eye was already swollen shut, and I could feel the bruises coming to the surface of my skin.

They swung the next door open and pushed me out, dropping me to the floor on my hands and knees once again.

With my good eye, I could see walls and walls of cells, and more stacked on top of each other.

We were on the ground floor, and I could see doors marked "Outside" and "Dining". It was all gray, and everything looked cold, heartless; not a single feeling of happiness seemed to exist in this place.

Blood pooled into my mouth, and I spat it out in front of me. I rubbed my nose with the back of my hand, smearing the remaining blood across my face. I took a deep and painful breath and slowly but surely, stood back up.

"Oh, we have a fighter here," someone yelled nearby. I looked around and found two arms hanging outside of their prison door, starting to slow clap for me. Great. I was already making amazing impressions.

Looking back at the officers, my eyes blurred them into one person. The man with the Gucci suit—the one who had beaten me after I spilled his coffee—appeared in their place... I blinked rapidly. Please... No. I couldn't be back there. I'd rather get pummeled by the police officers than restart in that station all over again. I rubbed my eyes in a panic before looking back up.

Officers *Limpy* and *Eyes* stood in front of me, *thankfully.* They shoved me forward, toward the end of the hall, past the outside and dining doors to the stairs. We started to climb them, each one more of a challenge to step up onto. After the third set, we walked down the aisle of cells and stopped about nineteen doors down.

They unlocked the cell in front of me and pushed me in. They threw me some toilet paper, a toothbrush, and toothpaste, all of it landing on the mangy ground before swinging the door shut. It echoed behind me. I didn't want to turn back to them.

"Kid," Officer *Eyes* called.

"Yeah?" I asked, hesitant.

"Come over here," he told me. I twisted slowly around and walked to the door.

"Stick your hands out so I can take off your cuffs."

I did what I was told, and he took them off. I'd been almost a hundred percent sure that he was going to give me another beating, but they must have got it all out downstairs. They had just made me walk up three flights in pain.

"Have fun in *hell!*" Officer *Eyes* yelled as he walked away, following Officer *Limpy* back down the stairs.

I turned back and didn't know what to think. I didn't know what to feel. I scooped up my stuff and placed it on what I guessed was my bed. It was thin, like paper thin, reminding me of the coldness back at the hospital.

There was a small, stained pillow placed on top of a dirty old blanket.

I sat down next to my new belongings and looked at the wall in front of me. There were marks everywhere—scratch marks, like someone thought they could escape by clawing their way out...

There was a stinky, disgusting, chrome toilet to the side and a small sink. And that just about did it for my house tour for the next seven and a bit years.

At least there was a small rectangle window at the very top of the back wall, which let in a sliver of light. *Great.* This was going to be *jussssst greatttt...*

*

My first day wasn't that bad. I was still here, in prison, which was a win in my eyes. My day could have been worse. *Like, I could have died.* I woke to an alarm blaring throughout the whole prison which was actually the breakfast bell.

I stood, a groan escaping me. I'd completely forgotten about the fight last night. I couldn't really call it a fight if I were being accurate. It was more like a one-sided beating, and I was just the punching bag. Still, better than being back at the station restarting over and over.

I gripped my middle tight, wrapping my sore arm firmly around, hugging myself, then walked out of my open door. It must have automatically opened at food times. I looked both ways before stepping out just like I was crossing a road. I really didn't want to crash into any oncoming traffic. It was all clear and I slowly made my way down the three sets of stairs.

On the ground floor, I found the door that led to the food hall thanks to a heavily armored guard standing outside of it. There was a line of people coming in and going out, so I hopped into the line that was going in.

Once I made it inside, it was basically a gym-sized prison cell. It did have more windows, but only at the tops of the walls. You'd have to sit on someone else's shoulders to be able to see out.

Getting caught up thinking about how to look out of the window was my first mistake. I walked into the back of someone, thinking the line was still moving. *It wasn't.*

I came face to face with one of the scariest-looking guys I think I've ever laid eyes on. And that's saying

210

something, since I grew up in one of the worst neighborhoods in New York.

"I hope someone pushed you into me," he said, as he turned around. His hair was long, matted, and greasy. He had face tattoos—a skull on his cheek and a few others that looked like they were written in Spanish. The tattoos trailed down his neck, and I assumed under his clothes. His eyes looked black— the darkest brown I'd even seen. By the time I'd thought of a reply, I probably had a hundred imaginary daggers stuck in me already.

"I'm really sorry," I said in a rush. I went to take a step back, but then I was no longer on the ground. His hand, which I swear was as big as my head, picked me up by my throat. Wind swooshed past me as I slammed down onto a nearby table, annoying the people eating their food who were now also angry with me.

"You need to watch where you're going, boy, or you won't last a week!" Skull face yelled. Spit splattered all over my face, but I dug my hands into his which was still wrapped around my neck.

"YOU HEAR ME, BOY? WATCH IT! OR NEXT TIME WILL BE YOUR LAST!" he screamed, letting me go and walking away like it was just another normal day in his life.

My hands were still at my throat as I slipped off the table and onto the floor. I kneeled, getting my breath back. I could feel everyone's eyes on me, watching me.

I decided to stand and walk slowly back into line. Everyone was still watching, their expressions all readable. I'd probably made the wrong choice, *my second mistake*.

When I finally got some food, I turned to the tables, but I couldn't find anywhere to sit. It was just like what I imagined starting at a new school would be like. Everyone spaced themselves out, not letting me sit anywhere.

So, you know where I sat? I sat at the very last table, at the very back of the room. Because, school logic: if you don't want to be seen, you try to blend into the background. ***It. Does. Not. Work. Like. That. In. Prison.*** I repeat, *it does not* work like that in prison.

I became a trash bin. Skull face was the first to drop his tray of crab onto me. Then everyone followed his cue.

After about twenty or so minutes, I was covered in a bunch of slop. I should have moved, but I couldn't be bothered.

The alarm went off again, and everyone filed out, back to their cells, just like I should have. But I wasn't sure how to move.

The alarm stopped, and everything went quiet. I slowly stood up when four guards walked through the door. They were all expressionless. *Robots.* They zoned in on me, and I swore under my breath.

The garbage peeled off me and fell to a heap on the floor. Two guards grabbed me by my arms, obviously forgetting or not caring about my shoulder. They dragged me away from the pile, the other two guards following behind.

They took me down a new corridor where we came to a new door. The "Shower room".

I ripped off my soaked-through jumpsuit, ignoring the crowd of guards watching. I stepped under the shower head, jumping back from the cold water hitting me. Why had I thought it would be warm water?

A splash hit me down by my feet. It was a block of soap the guards must have thrown at me. I picked it up and washed as fast I could, only getting used to the cold in the last few minutes before a guard pulled me out. He shoved a towel in my direction; it was the size of a hand towel? Seriously? They'd given me a hand towel?

I quickly dried myself and gave the towel back. Then one of the other *robot* guards gave me a new orange jumpsuit which I put on quickly. The four of them directed me out of the room and led me back to my cell.

Not a word was exchanged, the door clicking shut behind me.

I didn't think anything could have gone any worse, but then again, I did get a shower. I sat on my bed and stared at the wall once again, in complete silence.

*

A few hours later, another robot guard showed up at my door, unlocking it. All the guards wore the same uniform. It was almost as bad as my bright orange jumpsuit. They wore navy blue with a belt strapped around their middle and a black cap. Their belts held keys, handcuffs, and pepper spray. No name tags in sight, so I decided I was going to call this guard, *Scotty*.

Scotty told me, surprisingly not in a robotic voice, to put out my hands so he could handcuff me. He then led me down the steps and into another corridor that I hadn't seen on my arrival.

My eye was still pretty swollen, so it was a bit disorienting only seeing half of everything. *Scotty* showed me to a door, opening it and telling me to sit down at the chair across from a table. He then chained my handcuffs to the ground and left the room. *Goodbye then, Scotty.*

It was almost as if they were punishing me for the morning, even though I hardly provoked anything.

My mind changed once a man in a suit walked in. He looked clean; he looked like he could have worked anywhere else, but decided that he would try do a little good in the world and work with prisoners.

He didn't really have much hair left, and he wore glasses. He kind of looked like a middle-aged teacher. A concerned teacher.

"Hi, Joel, my name is David and I'm your counselor. I'll be asking you questions every day about how you're feeling, stuff like that, just to know you're not at risk," he said, taking a seat across from me.

"Risk of what?" I asked.

"Risk of suicide," David replied just as fast as me.

"Oh, because I haven't tried that before," I replied snarkily. *I'm tired, leave me be.*

"Look, Joel. I know you don't want to be here. But this is my job. You almost blew yourself up, making you a danger to others, and yourself. The court has ordered that you speak to a trained professional at least once a week, as well as prison. Since it said in your file you believe you tried to kill yourself, what? Nineteen times? You better buck up your ideas and let me help you."

He was a grumpy, *concerned* teacher.

"Fine," I said, letting him win.

"Okay, let's start, shall we?"

I nodded and let him continue.

"How are you feeling today?" He took out his notepad, ready to write my answer.

"Like a piece of shirt." I don't bother to look up at his face. I can already tell what it would look like since I didn't actually swear.

"Do you feel this way because you feel guilty about your actions?"

"I suppose so. Also, two officers beat the fork out of me and then this tattoo guy strangled me," I told him.

"… Mmm, I'll have a talk to security about that," David mumbled.

"Will you or are you just saying that to make me feel better?" I asked.

"Does it make you feel better?" David asked. *Was he for real? Did he just say that?*

"No, Dan. Daniel. Whatever the hell your name is. You can't just mumble a reply and move on. Treat me like a human being. Not like a dog. I have feelings. I didn't THINK I WOULD BE HERE!" I yelled, suddenly out of breath.

David looked away from his notepad, surprised. He didn't expect it to go like this, obviously. "Joel, I'm going to have to ask you to calm down," he said in such a counselor voice.

"You know why else I feel like a piece of shirt?" I asked him.

"Why, Joel? Tell me why!" he said, suddenly interested—he even physically leaned in.

"Because I feel guilty, not just about blowing innocent people up. I feel guilty because I'm thankful that I have a second chance at life. And she doesn't," I said.

"Who doesn't?" he asked, like he didn't already know.

"I've had enough. I just want to go to bed."

Livvie's face blurred in my mind. She was right there, but I couldn't quite see her. I wanted to see her. My rage was consuming my hope. I needed to get a handle on my anger, otherwise I was never going to get through this.

"Okay… well, I'll see you tomorrow. Guard?" David stood, walking up to the door and knocking. It opened, letting him out.

Scotty fetched me soon after and put me back in my cell. An hour or two later—I had no idea of what time it was anymore—the alarm went off again. I was still so disoriented.

I watched everyone's doors open except mine. I wasn't allowed to go to dinner, probably because of the scene I accidentally caused during breakfast… I screamed out in anger. I was stuck in this forkin' concrete box. And what was even worse was that I was hungry. And everyone knows, hunger feeds ***rage.***

Chapter Forty

Time in prison was no longer just a concept. Prison worked off a *whole* different schedule. Honestly, it felt similar when I was stuck back at the station. I almost did the exact same thing every day… except, well I was still alive, and the days did change a little. I do keep wondering why I was still alive or why I hadn't restarted yet, but I guess it could be because I took the vest off myself. I made the decision to keep living…

I'd been locked away a whole week, and I almost wanted to celebrate it as some sort of anniversary. I needed cake.

I felt so crazy, maybe I could fulfill having a psychotic break.

Prison worked like this:

Sleep.

Breakfast alarm.

Back to cells.

Outside alarm (only on Tuesdays, Thursdays, and Saturdays in the winter, but I'd been told it would be every day in summer—I couldn't wait!).

Brown paper bag lunch in our cells.

Guard came and got me for my counselling sessions. David said he'd come every day for the first month, and then he'd drop to once a week. Apparently, we were making good process.

Dinner alarm.

Back to cells for sleep.

I had *such* a busy life.

I never knew the actual time. I guessed breakfast was around eight in the morning, and dinner must've been at about six or seven at night. Otherwise, I had no idea.

I kept my head down and managed to avoid any further beatings. Other inmates that seemed around my age sometimes let me sit with them but only occasionally. At least *that* was something.

My eye had healed a little—the swelling had gone down, and I could see out of it again. The other bruises were fading too. That was one way to mark the passing of time, I guessed.

My shoulder… well, that wasn't healing. My arm still hung limp by my side, perhaps because they had taken the sling away. It made me angry every time I looked at it. It was another reminder of all the stupid decisions I've made.

Well, today something different finally happened. I got called to the visitors' room and told someone wanted to talk to me.

"Lewis, you have a visitor," a guard said outside my cell door. He brought me out of my thoughts. It must have been Dufty.

The door beeped above me before the automatic locks unlatched and it swayed open. I walked with the guard until we reached the visitors' room, and he pushed me inside. It was filled with *robot* security guards on each wall. Except the far wall. That was made up of little booths which each had their own phone, their own stool and a little desk facing a plexiglass wall. On the other side, I assumed was the same set-up.

It took me a moment to see Dufty, but when I did, my heart dropped. He would be… he must be so ashamed of me. How could I talk to him? We only had fifteen minutes, and I'd already wasted two of them by gawking at him.

A guard gave me a shove in Dufty's direction, so I went and sat down in the booth in front of him. I looked down at my hands. I did not want him to see me like this. The poor man probably thought he *had* to come see me.

A plastic-sounding knock brought me out of my thoughts, and I jerked my head up to see Dufty being told off by a security guard on his side. He shrugged the warning off and pointed at the phone.

I looked at it, then back at him. He nodded eagerly, so I picked up the receiver as if it were a glass ballerina. Putting it to my ear, I heard his voice.

"Joel, my boy," Dufty said, sounding out of breath. I looked down again, guilt eating my insides.

"... Hey, Dufty," I said awkwardly.

"Joel, look at me. Look at me, son," Dufty said softly. Slowly raising my head, tears brimmed in my eyes.

He touched the plastic screen. His palm stretched out, reaching for mine. "Son, it's okay," he told me again, almost choking over his words. I raised my hand to his, gently placing mine against the screen. I could no longer hold my tears in; they spilled out, uncontrollably.

"It's okay; I understand. I should have been there for you, and Olivia." Dufty said, choking on his own words.

"It's not okay. Look at me, I'm a mess. I tried to murder innocent people! How can you stand me? How are you even here?" my voice came out hoarse, my vision going blurry.

"Listen to me, I should've seen the signs. I should have helped you. You needed help. You didn't know how else to end your suffering. I'm here now. I'm here, okay, son?"

"But... but why?" I asked him.

"You and Liv walked into my shop. You both looked helpless. You asked for a job, and that's all I could give you at the time. And I wish I could have given you so much more—"

"You did," I interrupted. "You always gave me more than what I earned. You did help us, and I can't burden you with asking for anything more now," I wanted to hug him so much, it hurt. I needed to show him how much he had helped me. Helped *us.*

"I should've known that you two needed more than money. I should have known," Dufty continued.

"Please don't. You did help us," I told him. He **needed** to understand that.

"Let me help you now, then," he said with determination.

I didn't even consider "no" as an answer. "Dufty…"

"I'll come as much as I can. At least once a month. We will make plans for after you get out. Let me help you. You need someone, Joel. You don't have to be alone," he pleaded.

"I… I couldn't let you do that," I told him. I was already in debt with him.

"Too bad. It's going to happen," he said, and I couldn't argue with him.

"You don't have to," I told him again.

"Nope. No. I'm going to be here for you," he said, stubborn as ever.

"Dufty—" I started, but he cut me off.

"Shush. Let me help you. Let's start with who gave you that nasty black eye. I'll have a talk to someone out here," he said, turning to look at a guard leaning on a wall behind him.

"No!" I yelled down the phone. "Uh, no, I mean. You can't do that. I'm trying to avoid another beating. And I don't think that'll help. Thank you, though."

"Fine, but if I show up next time and you look the same, I will be talking to someone."

"No one will care," I told him.

"I do," he said, and I could already see him making a plan in his head.

"Thank you." I smiled at him, taking my hand away and wiping my eyes with the back of it.

Someone tapped me on the shoulder. I followed the hand up to a security guard mouthing "time's up" to me. I took the phone away from my ear, now holding it between my hands.

"Please… please give me two more minutes," I begged him.

"Nope, off you go," he said.

"Please, I need to tell him that—"

Robot guard grabbed my shirt and pulled me up. I was still holding the phone tightly between my hands, and I kicked out with my leg, making him let go.

"I love you, Dufty. I always thought of you as my dad, and I can't—"

The phone ripped out of my hands as I heard Dufty yell through the plastic screen. Two guards were now on me, hauling me up like I was nothing,

"I CAN'T THANK YOU ENOUGH!" I yelled, while being dragged out the door.

They dropped me outside and folded their arms, guarding the door back to the phones. Standing up, I brushed off the dust, scowling at them.

"Kid, if I were you, I would follow the rules before you get beaten to a pulp. Just a warning," one of the guards said. Maybe they weren't all robots.

I backed away, knocking into another guard who grabbed me by the shoulders. I almost screamed from the pain that rippled through me, but I bit down on my lip making it bleed. He then directed me away and back to my cell.

That could have gone worse. I thought the guards *were* gonna give me an example of what pulp was…

Chapter Forty-One

December 5th, 2008
One month later

Dufty kept his word, and a month later I was called to the phone room again. We talked about how his coffeehouse was going, and the idea of going back to work with him after my seven years.

Nothing else really happened. I kept to myself, and no one tried to pick on me. There were other new guys that came in and were given the same abuse I received in the first week. I could move my shoulder around a little bit now, and I kind of tried giving myself physio for it.

It was pretty boring. *Not gonna lie*—the food wasn't very good, and I was struggling with being around men, twenty-four seven. The only exciting thing that happened was David, my counselor, coming and trying to pry into my life. He thought it was helping, but I could neither agree nor disagree. He came less regularly now, instead of every day, it was just once a week.

I made my way to my last session for the month. The guards seemed to have eased up on me, and they weren't so bad, but they still looked like robots that hated their jobs.

One guard led me into the same room David and I usually talked in, and I plopped down in the chair by the table. He was waiting for me and gave me a small smile before beginning. David took the time and date, writing them down in his notes before he started with his usual questions.

"How are you, Joel?" He always used my name when he asked me questions, so sometimes I called him Daniel to be annoying, like he was.

"Just dandy, Daniel," I said. He *loved* my sarcastic replies. I could feel the heat in the room rise. *He loved me, hah.*

"Joel, if you want to show any progress for the parole board, you should take this seriously. I won't be telling you again," he said, threatening me.

"Fine. I'm bored," I told him.

"Thank you. Why are you bored?" David said, writing down a few notes.

"I sleep. I eat. Repeat. I think I'm becoming more mentally insane by doing nothing."

"Okay, I'll look into something for you." David said, nodding.

"Mm-hm. And how are you?" I asked.

"Oh…" He looked up, shocked, like no one had ever asked him that before. "I'm good, thanks. Thank you for asking."

"Cool."

"So, I brought in some photos today for you to look at." He moved the images across the table. "I want you to tell me what you think of them."

"Sure." I picked them up and looked at the first one. It was a picture of the sky, and a cloud that looked like a tree. "A tree."

"Okay, keep going."

The next one was of a nuclear family, parents behind their kids, all smiling.

"They look happy," I said.

"Mm-hm keep going."

I looked at the next photo, and it was almost the same, except... except, *was that my dad?*

"Is this some cruel joke or something?" I demanded, throwing the photos back on the table.

"What do you mean, Joel?" He wanted me to admit I recognized the man in the second photo. He looked happy as well, like he was enjoying his life. He had kids, and I assumed the lady next to him was his wife. That betrayer.

"No, I'm not doing this." I went to fold my arms over my chest, forgetting my wrists were handcuffed.

"Do what, Joel?"

"This!" I tried to gesture at the photos thrown over the table and failed due to the same reason I couldn't fold my arms. *These stupid, stupid handcuffs.* At least my handcuffs were no longer chained to the ground like they used to be.

"What did you see, Joel?"

227

"MY DAD!" Ahh fork, I'd admitted it.

"And?"

"Why are you showing me this?" I said, ready to crumple into myself.

"I was curious about why you've never asked about him, never tried to find him," David said.

"He left us," I told him.

"That doesn't mean you couldn't have gone and found him?"

"Dad... my dad didn't know what to do. I was seven... maybe six? I can't remember." I could remember.

"Why did he leave?"

"Mom. She... she was abusive. He was only trying help her, but he stopped trying. He could have taken us with him." May as well admit everything.

"Why do you think he left you?"

I don't know. "We reminded him too much of Mom, probably..." I said.

"And where is your mom now, Joel?" David asked.

"Can we not?" I spat at him. My eyes felt like they were on fire. *Why did we have to talk about this stuff?*

"I'm trying to help you, Joel," he looked up from his notes, finally noticing how much distress he was putting me through.

"You're torturing me," I said in a low growl. If he said my name one more time, I was going to lose it.

"That wasn't my intention."

Was he a robot now too?

"Mom is probably dead; I have no idea. I'm glad Dad decided to remove us from his memory and start again. Good. For. Him," I said sourly.

"And where is your sister?"

The prick! *How could he not know?* He should have already read my file by now.

I let a moment of silence pass. David's knee started to bounce. Maybe he didn't believe the files… Was he nervous of my answer? Did he think I killed her or something?

Maybe I could tell the truth and scare the hell out of him. Why not? Surely, he already knew. I looked him straight in the eye and spoke in a deathly calm voice.

"She's dead, she had the flu, which turned into pneumonia, and she drowned in her own liquid. I didn't even realize it was that bad, and of course, Mom didn't even notice she was sick…"

It felt like she was right there; I could see her in front of me.

"I didn't take her to the doctor. I was scared of CPS removing her, but I should have let them. She would have been better off far away from us."

"That must have really taken a toll on you Joel, I'm beginning to understand how you got into your situation—"

I cut him off. "If you watched the news, you would have already known," I told him.

"You're right. I did know. But for you to tell me that, it's actually showing me that you're progressing," he told me, turning back to his notepad.

"I've had enough of you for today, Daniel," I said, biting my tongue to stop myself hurling abuse his way.

"It's David. Don't you want to know what happened to your mom?" he asked. I paused for a second wondering whether he was joking.

"Sure," I muttered.

"The cops searched your place just in case you had any other explosive devices sitting around at home and didn't find any traces of your mom. She must've heard them coming and ran away or something. No one can find her. Would you have any idea where she would go?" he asked.

The police must have told him to ask; it seemed weird to bring it up otherwise. I wasn't really shocked that she'd run away, though maybe she didn't run away. Maybe she was just out. I shrugged. I didn't care anymore.

I stood from my chair and walked toward the door, without even a goodbye. The guard opened it and followed me back to my cell. He undid my handcuffs and walked away. I was alone. I was always alone.

I flopped down onto my paper-thin bed and looked up at the ceiling.

The past isn't all bad. You had some of your best memories there. Livvie. Livvie was there and she was filled with hope, I told myself. *Give me hope, Livvie.*

Help. Me. Be. Like. You.

Chapter Forty-Two

"How are you feeling today, Joel?" David asked.

It had been a whole year since we started these sessions; since I'd been in prison. And if I was honest, life had only gotten better. I'd grown a full beard and I'd actually muscled up a bit.

I didn't have any prison tats, and I didn't plan on getting any unless it was against my will. I'd actually won a few prison brawls, *which I'd never intended on starting.* Some of the new inmates actually *"respected"* me. I had a few buddies, who I sat with during mealtimes, and we chatted. We rarely had anything to talk about, it was mostly just nonsense stories. No one in their right mind would ever believe them.

I tried to help some of the newer inmates out by giving them a quick run-down of how everything worked, something I wished someone would have done for me.

The other day there was this guy in the showers; he was muffling his cries with the shower noise, but I could hear him, meaning *everyone* could also hear him. And he would have got serious shirt about it if I hadn't stepped in. Got a bit of a beating myself because of it, but still, prison is hard to adjust to.

It wasn't all good, but it could have been worse. Dufty still came to see me monthly. He was actually the only thing keeping me sane. He was doing well, looking older every time I saw him, and he told me all about his new granddaughter who was recently born. Dufty brought new photos to show me through the plastic screen; it made me happy seeing him happy. His little granddaughter reminded me of Livvie—she had big brown eyes filled with wonder.

Livvie hadn't been on my mind as much as she used to be. I still missed her every day. *Every second of every day I missed her,* but the sad thing was, I was finally getting used to missing her.

I'd been noticing small things that reminded me of her throughout the day, such as the sunlight streaming through the small windows, spreading out across the floor, trying to reach as far as it could, trying to reach all the dark corners. And when I stood in it, I felt warm, and I could imagine Livvie wrapping me up in one of her little hugs.

"Joel?" David interrupted my thoughts and looked at me with worry.

"Huh?" I replied, my voice groggy. I wiped at my eyes, swiping away the tears that were starting.

"How are you? Are you alright, Joel?" he leaned forward a little as if he was trying to get a better look at me.

"How many times have I told you, Daniel, you don't need to end every question with my name."

"It's David."

"I know."

"Don't ignore my question, Joe, how are you?"

"Did you... Did you just call me Joe? *Ugh, whatever*. I'm fine, just the usual. How are you?" I asked him.

"So how come you were just crying?"

"You don't miss a beat, do you?" I replied, annoyance now lacing my voice.

"Nope, this is my job," David replied. He pushed himself back into his chair and rested his feet on the table that sat between us. I was pretty sure I was one of his easiest clients, so he was a bit more laid back when it came to our sessions.

"The sun makes me feel like Livvie is hugging me," I admitted, shyness taking over me. I looked down.

"When did this start?" he asked, writing down a note.

"Probably after a month into my prison sentence."

"Why, Joel?" David dropped from his propped-up position, now looking more serious.

"I guess I was struggling, so I found a little happiness," I said, looking back up at him.

"That's good to hear, Joel." He scribbled something else.

"Mm-hm. Anyway, how have you been?" I asked again.

"Not bad, not bad. My wife just had a baby boy, so we haven't been sleeping much at all."

I was pretty sure he wasn't meant to talk about his personal life to any prison inmates, but he must be making an exception, just for me.

"Congrats, man, but is that why you seem like you can't really be bothered with today's session?" I asked, a teasing tone now lacing my voice instead of the annoyance from earlier.

"No, no, that's not it—"

"You're just tired?" I said, interrupting him.

"No. Yes. Look—"

"You want me to cause a scene, so I get taken back to my cell earlier so you can go home and sleep?" I interrupted again.

"No, I never asked that. I—"

Before he could finish, I stood suddenly, alerting the guard stationed outside the door. The guard turned around and fumbled with the lock. His forehead creased with panic.

"I DON'T WANT YOUR HELP!" I yelled at the top of my lungs. I could see a slight grin forming on David's face. I decided to go all out and kick my chair out behind me. It made a loud clang, echoing around the room.

The door swung open, and the guard rushed in. He moved past the chair and pushed me by the shoulders until I hit the wall.

"Calm down, Joel," David said, now standing up. He walked over to the guard, pulling his shoulder back. It did nothing.

"HOW MANY TIMES DID I SAY TO STOP USING MY NAME AT THE END OF QUESTIONS?" I yelled through a gritted smile.

The guard raised his arm and pressed it into the back of my neck. David went to pull the guard back, but before he could, another guard appeared and shoved him out of the way.

The two guards threw me forward, the handcuffs making it impossible to brace for the floor, which greeted me a few seconds later. David swore over my shoulder but was too slow to act. The guards were already hauling me up and pushing me out the door, closing it behind me. They moved me down the corridor before throwing me up the first set of stairs. I landed awkwardly, my hip taking the full impact.

Before I could stand, they picked me up again, my feet barely touching the ground as we climbed the two other floors to my cell.

They finally let go just outside my cell door. One stood staunchly while the other unlocked it. He seemed to be fumbling with his keys, like before. Was he scared of me? I was a twig, compared to him.

"Boo!" I yelled at him. I probably should have thought that through, but I couldn't help myself.

The guard almost jumped out of his skin causing me to let out a small laugh, before the staunch guard pushed me forward into my now opened cell. Just my luck, though, I never heard the door behind me shut. I started to turn around, but I didn't make it very far. A searing heat hit me across the side of my face before I felt the cool mattress on my other side.

Chapter Forty-Three

October 23rd, 2016
Six and a half years later

Staring out the door, it didn't feel real. I was finally leaving. My sentence was finally done. I was done. I was free, and I almost didn't feel ready to leave. This place, as much as it had hurt me, it had also helped with fixing me. I hadn't felt more like me in years.

I looked out through the window next to the door, only seeing my reflection looking back at me. I looked worn out and tired, and I was pale. My eyes were a darker brown than I remembered, and so was my hair, probably from the reduced amount of sun I'd gotten. I had a week's growth of stubble. Thankfully we had a grooming session a week ago, and my hair wasn't too long. The ends were curling up though, and the top was just fluffy.

I wasn't as scrawny as when I started my sentence, which was nice. I'd muscled up a little bit thanks to boredom. Sometimes I would do pushups until my arms decided to stop functioning.

I was dressed in the same clothes I'd come in with—gray sweats, my old Nikes and a gray hoodie. They were all a bit tight now, considering back in the hospital, they almost swallowed me up whole. It was definitely better than my bright orange jumpsuit, though.

My hand hovered over the doorknob; I felt too scared to leave. What if I stepped outside and had the biggest mental breakdown someone could have? Or would I be completely fine? The anxiety rattled through me, making me jittery.

Maybe I should go back and ask them if they got the date right. Out of all the days, it just had to be this one. It had been eight years since she died. Eight years without my little sidekick, and look where I was now, still standing in front of a door, contemplating whether I'd rather live in the world or in prison.

Dufty was probably waiting for me, and I should probably leave, but that would mean… it would mean I'd have to start doing things. Specifically, *living*.

"Livvie, give me strength," I whispered under my breath.

"Joel?" Someone called my name, making me almost jump out of my skin.

"Ahh! You scared me," I moved away from the door and faced them. "Oh, it's you."

"Is that all? *Oh, it's you?* After all the time we've spent together, come on," David said with a grin on his face. We'd actually become good buddies over the years of counselling. I didn't know he was going to be here today, otherwise I probably would have left as fast as I could. I was predicting a raid of questions coming my way in three, two, on—

"Is the door too hard to open, Joel?" he asked, curiosity taking over his expression.

He stood there with a to-go coffee in his hand. This was the first time I'd ever been in front of him out of my prison clothes and wearing no handcuffs. I took a little step back, suddenly afraid about all the shirt I gave him over the years. Maybe that was why he'd turned up today.

"Earth to Joel? Hello? You alright? Do you need to sit down? Joel?" David reached out to touch my shoulder, but I flinched away.

"Give me a second," I said. I closed my eyes and took a slow but controlled breath in and out, just like David taught me to do when I got too overwhelmed. He'd said this might happen once I got out of prison. I could feel him take a step back, giving me space before I reopened my eyes.

"I'm sorry, I shouldn't have bombarded you with questions. I should have known that this would be overwhelming for you—we literally just talked about it last month."

"It's alright, David," I told him.

"I'm sorry. Is there anything I can help you with?"

"You could open the door for me…" I asked, hesitantly.

"Sure, but why can't you?"

We both looked at the doorknob, waiting for it to answer. Its silver gleam just stared at us in return.

Sighing, I decided to answer honestly. "I can physically; I'm just having trouble doing it mentally."

"And why is that, Joel?"

"Daniel. We've talked about using my name at the end of your questions." I let out a little laugh, and so did he. I was pretty sure he just said it to calm the air between us. "There's the whole world out there, and I don't know if I'm ready."

"I think you are," David said with certainty.

"How do you know? I'll have to start *living*."

"Joel, when I first met you, you were a confused eighteen-year-old lost in the world. Over the years, I've seen your kindness, helping the other inmates out. You stand up for what you believe in. You have been living, even if it hasn't been what you imagined it would be. I know losing Olivia was hard, but I also think what you went through has made you a better person," David said.

This was the most honest David had ever been with me. He looked shyly down at his feet. He'd always been a matter-of-fact kinda guy, but now I realized he actually cared, and he had listened to me.

Tears formed in my eyes, and I stepped toward him, cautiously. He didn't take a step away; he wasn't scared of me, which made me smile. Tears now ran down my cheeks, and I wasn't embarrassed by them; I embraced them. I wrapped my arms around David and gave him a hug—a sign of thanks. I didn't know where I would be without him. It took David a moment to respond before I could feel his hands pat me in return.

"Thank you. You have helped me probably more than I've shown," I told him. I backed out of the hug and looked at the doorknob again. Out of the corner of my eye, I saw his hand rise to wipe his own eyes.

"Thank you. Now let's do this. You're ready," he told me.

"Okay, okay, let's do this." I rolled my shoulders back and cracked my neck before grabbing onto the doorhandle. It was cold to the touch, and I felt myself pulling away from it, until David wrapped his hand around mine. I let out a big breath and twisted it clockwise, pushing it forward.

An icy wind greeted me, sending shivers down my spine. I lifted my lead-heavy leg up and took a step outside. Then another and another, and before I realized, I was running. I was running with no direction in mind. *I was free.*

"Joel! This way to the carpark!" David yelled from behind me.

I looked behind and saw him pointing to the right with a massive grin on his face. I changed direction, now running toward the parking lot. I yelled a thanks toward David, who had started to chuckle to himself.

I had no idea what Dufty's car looked like, but thankfully I could see a little old man leaning on the hood of his champagne-colored car. He wore a dress shirt and dress pants, as if he had to impress me. The little hair he had left was combed over and soon would be covered up with the retro Dodgers baseball cap he held in his hands. He was shorter than I remembered.

He looked off to the side, unaware of my approach. I ran faster toward him, catching his attention. Dufty's face lit up, and he smiled at me with warmth and familiarity.

"JOEL!" he yelled, a second before I clashed into him, giving him the biggest hug I could muster. He squeezed me back just as tight, just as I would imagine a father would.

I leaned back and looked at him. It was Dufty. *My Dufty.* He raised his hands and smooshed my face, kissing me on both cheeks like the true Italian New Yorker he was.

"I missed you, my son," he said in his thick accent before letting go of me. He moved around his car, an old Nissan Maxima, probably from the early 2000s.

"I missed you too," I said, before opening the car door on my side, noticing paint chipping away around the edges. Dufty jumped into the driver's seat, and I slipped into the passenger side. We smiled at each other again, and he started up the engine. We had nothing new to say, since we'd seen each other monthly for the last seven years.

"What took you so long?" Dufty asked, reversing out of the parking space.

"I had trouble opening the door," I replied sheepishly.

"Prisons these days, everything is broken. They need to get onto that," he said, nodding his head. There was a slight tease to his voice, but I didn't tell him that the door worked perfectly fine. I could tell he knew it was about more than the physical door. I wasn't sure how I knew this; I just did. It was Dufty; of course he knew.

"Where are we going?" I asked, only just noticing that we'd left the prison grounds. It was a beautiful day. The blue sky surrounded us, with no clouds in sight. Fall colors draped everything, giving the cold, crisp air a sense of warmth through the browns and oranges.

"Home. We're going home," Dufty said, turning his head to look at me instead of the road. There were tears in his eyes, and his smile was so big it took up most of his face.

"Thank you, Dufty. Thank you for everything." I smiled. I couldn't have been happier.

Chapter Forty-Four

The blue sky dimmed the further we drove into New York. Once we were fully in the city, stuck behind other cars, horns blaring and people trying to change lanes last minute, I finally felt that I was almost home. Surprisingly, I'd missed the busyness, and I felt a sense of comfort come over me, helping me to relax more into the passenger seat.

Dufty had caught me up on everything that had changed during the years I was in prison. To sum it up, I hadn't missed much. Except Dufty's coffee bar had been re-painted, so that was something.

We were getting nearer to my old neighborhood. I knew the streets like I knew the back of my hand, even now. We drove past a street where I could see a young boy and girl riding on their bike. The little girl sat on the handlebars and the fall leaves flew around them. She lifted her hands up, trying to pop them as if they were *bubbles*...

I accidentally swore out loud. I turned around, twisting in my seat belt to have a better look. Thanks to the traffic, we hadn't passed the street yet.

"You alright, son?" Dufty asked me.

I ignored him and strained my neck to look back. We started to crawl forward. I couldn't see the kids anymore; it was as if they had vanished. *Did I just imagine them? Was it Livvie and me? Maybe I need to go to a mental asylum next...*

"Son?" Dufty brought me back to reality by laying his hand on my shoulder. He glanced back and forth between the road in front of him and me.

"Oh... it's nothing. I just thought I saw something," I said, already slouching back into my seat. I was sure it was her... but I must have imagined it.

"You sure?" Dufty looked at me, now curious.

"Yeah, don't worry about it."

"Only if you're sure."

"I'm sure," I said looking back out the window.

"Mm-hm." Dufty turned his attention to the road. "We're almost there anyway," he said, flicking on his turn signal.

Fall leaves covered the ground and the car blew them around, bringing the memory back up to the surface. I shook it out of my mind as Dufty slowed down and pulled onto the side of the road, shifting the car into park.

I wasn't sure what I was expecting; it was just a basic New York townhouse. It looked a little run down, but it was better than what I grew up in. Its red bricks had taken on a gray tint, and the stairs up to the door were covered in a green moss which I assumed would be slippery. I guessed that's why the railing on the stairs looked so steady. I set a little mental note to hold onto it when going up the steps.

"You coming, Joel?" Dufty knocked me out of my thoughts once again. He'd gotten out and grabbed my few belongings from the back seat.

I wasn't sure where he'd got those from though. Had the police released them to him?

He knocked on my window again, smiling at me with warmth. I unclicked my seat belt and hopped out, suddenly feeling very scruffy.

I'd never met his wife before, and my nerves prickled. I wondered whether she was okay with this arrangement.

Dufty had offered me his guest room and a job back at his twenty-four-hour coffee bar while I sorted myself out. *Sorted what?* I asked myself as the front door started opening. I held onto the railing, a step down from Dufty. I felt like I was back all those years ago, asking Dufty for a job, shyness overtaking me.

"Joel, this is my Sofia," Dufty said, introducing me to his wife, after giving her a quick hug.

My eyes traveled from her feet to her face slowly. She wore slippers, tight jeans, a big stripy cardigan, and her arms were crossed. I wouldn't have been surprised if she started tapping her foot. Her hair stopped at her shoulders, and it was gray. She was little, almost half my height. My eyes finally reached her face. It was soft. Years of hard work showed on her skin, but she was smiling, a warm smile like

Dufty's. Her eyes were a soft amber color and they looked compassionate.

"Presto vieni dentro, si gela." She spoke quickly, and she reached her arm out to me, pulling me inside before Dufty closed the door behind us. *"Si gela, hai freddo?"* she said looking me up and down before shaking her head.

Was she speaking Italian?

"Dufty? *Sta per ammalarsi, dev'essere congelato. Prendi alcuni dei tuoi vestiti,"* she asked him.

"Si, si," Dufty replied, waving her off before moving up the stairs slowly. Definitely Italian.

Sofia pulled me away from the front door and into their living room. She basically pushed me down onto the couch before rummaging around in a cupboard nearby. She brought me a blanket and laid it on my lap before quickly walking away, around a corner to what I assumed was their kitchen. The living room curtains were pulled, making it dark; the soft orange light above me hardly helping at all.

Their furniture was old, I guessed from the seventies era… better than none though, and the air smelled like coffee grounds, like Dufty's coffee bar. It comforted me.

"Joel? Want coffee? Yes?" Sofia yelled out to me. Her accent was thick, but at least I knew what she was saying now.

"Yes! *Si!"* I replied. I had no idea why I said yes back in Italian; it just happened. My cheeks heated with embarrassment. I almost face-palmed when I heard her quick footsteps returning.

She handed me a cup and saucer and laid a plate of cheese and crackers on the table in front of us, taking a seat next to me. She also brought herself some coffee.

"So, Joel," she started. She said my name with a "g" sound and ended it with a "le". *It. Was. Cute.*

"Yes, ma'am?" I looked up, taking a quick sip of her bland coffee. It mostly just tasted like milk. I had to focus on my expression after sipping, so I didn't make one that would offend her.

"Joel," she paused for a moment, and my heart sank a little.

I knew I wouldn't be welcome.

"You stay as long as you want. Ask if you need anything, yes? *Si?*" Sofia said, before nodding and taking a sip of her own coffee.

I couldn't help but smile at her. I was so thankful.

"Thank you so much, Sofia. How do you say thank you in Italian?" I asked. If I was going to live there, I thought I should at least attempt to learn what she was saying half the time.

"Grazie," she said, already smiling at me.

"Grazie!" I said, happiness filling my voice. Dufty's heavy footsteps came down the stairs, and he walked around the corner looking at the both of us with curiosity.

"You're teaching him without me? Sofiaaaa. *Hai detto che l'averemmo fatto insieme!"* He sounded

exasperated and a smile tugged at his lips. Sofia let
out a little laugh, and I watched them interact for a
moment. They looked totally still in love.

"I think I'll have to learn faster if every second word
you say I can't understand!" I said.

A chuckle escaped Dufty, causing all three of us to
break into a fit of laughter.

*

The night escaped us. I ended up moving into their
small kitchen, sitting at their very old and used oak
dining table, watching Sofia and Dufty cook together.
They made ravioli, even making the pasta by hand. I
was completely mesmerized by them.

It was a piece of beauty watching them giggle like a
newly married couple, listening to an old radio play
songs in the background, their glasses of wine off to
the side.

The conversations flowed like water, no bumps
along the way. Not once. And not once was there a
question about my family or my past, except a few
memories Dufty and I brought up about working at
his coffeehouse.

The ravioli was a literal dream in my mouth. I'd
forgotten such food existed outside of prison. I was so
used to eating slop every day, I forgot to miss actual
food. I basically siphoned it; I was eating so fast Sofia
slapped me on the hand, giving me a fright.

"*Rallentare! Assaggiarlo!* Slow down! Taste it! Goodness me, *boi*." Sofia shook her head, looking down at her plate of food, trying to hide her smile. I stopped eating like I was starving and that's when the flavors exploded in my mouth. It was the best thing I'd ever tasted. I happily accepted seconds, and after that was finished, I was tempted to ask for thirds, but zipped my mouth shut. Instead, I collected our plates and brought them to the counter where I started to rinse them.

It was probably close to ten at night by then; I wasn't sure since I still needed to pick up a phone. I found a clock on the oven and looked at it twice, second guessing what I was reading. It was actually twenty-five minutes before midnight. *Ouch.* I was wondering why my body had been quietly requesting sleep for the past four hours now.

"What are you doing, son?" Dufty asked, coming up behind me and taking the scrubbing brush out of my hand.

"The dishes?" I replied, puzzled.

"Guests don't do the dishes," he told me.

"Technically, I'm not your guest; you're letting me live with you, Dufty. Let me do the dishes," I said. A smile spread across my face as we started to wrestle over the scrubbing brush. "Come on, it's the least I can do. *Grazia*, again, Sofia. Dinner was delicious," I said, looking back at her. She winked at me.

"Don't you suck up to her, and guests max out in a week. Then you can start helping with chores," Dufty replied, snatching the scrubbing brush out of my hand.

"Hey! Give that back!" I lunged forward reaching for the brush, fully committing, except I should have known better. Dufty caught me around the middle, picking me up and dropping me outside of the kitchen.

"Don't you dare say: *'woah old man you still have it'*, otherwise I'll sit on you, *mascalzone!"* he said, already laughing at the shocked expression that had plastered itself over my face. I was a head taller than him and no doubt heavier. How on earth did that just happen?

"Didn't Dufty ever tell you he was a wrestler back in Italy before we moved over here? Have you not noticed the photos?" Sofia said in between her laughter.

She moved her hand around, gesturing to the walls. She was right, I hadn't noticed the photos that lined them. I was too focused on her and Dufty—on watching a normal life scenario.

I stood and dusted my pants off. I moved from one photo to the next. There were pictures of Sofia and Dufty when they were first married, old wrestling photos, their children's photos—two boys and a girl. There was one of their new granddaughter that Dufty always talked about, and shots of Dufty's coffee bar. Their whole life story was on these walls. I wanted to go into every room and search for every photo, but somehow, I was being steered up the stairs. More and more photos lined the walls, but I was being torn away from them.

"Joel? You alright?" Dufty brought me out of my trance. He opened a door in front of me and walked in, flicking the light on. The same orange glow lit up around the room, the wallpaper looking old and ripped in some places.

"Sorry about this. I was going to make it nice for you, but yeah… this was the boys' room, and we knew better so… yeah, sorry about it." Dufty almost sounded ashamed.

I stepped in, looking around, already feeling more at home than I had in years. "No, no, it's great. Thank you so much," I said.

"It's nothing. You gotta stop with the thank yous; you're spoiling Sofia." Dufty made his way over to the cupboard in the corner of the room. He shut it gently, but it opened again, just a smidgen.

"It is more than enough," I said, sighing. I took a seat on the edge of the bed. It was soft. It wasn't flat, it wasn't hard, it was nothing like the prison beds. I couldn't believe it; I started to cry.

"Hey, hey, Joel, what's wrong?" Dufty said, sitting down next to me. He reached into his pocket and took out a pack of tissues, giving me one. I couldn't help but let out a little laugh before wiping my eyes and blowing my nose. I was a grown man. I was twenty-six, and I was crying over a bed. Who was I?

"Oh, it's nothing, this bed is amazing," I said.

"You crying about a bed? My goodness, son, prison made you soft!" Dufty said, gently punching me in the shoulder.

"Yeah, yeah, I know," I said with a shrug.

"Is it about anything else?"

"What do you mean?" I asked.

"Well, when my daughter used to cry—and she was a dramatic one—she used to say, 'I was crying about one thing, but now I'm crying about everything', then all hell would break loose. You should have seen it! It was a show," he said, shaking his head at the memory.

It made sense to me, though. This evening had been surreal to me. It had been overwhelming, and I hadn't felt this loved in many, many years. So maybe I was crying for more than one reason.

"That makes sense," I told him.

"Does it?" he asked.

"Yeah. I guess I was beginning to cry about a lot of other things too. I started wondering what my mom and dad are up to. The photos on your walls must hold so many memories. And so does this bedroom, look at all the scuff marks. And tonight has been amazing; I haven't felt this loved in years…" *Please let this be real. Please don't restart; this has to be real, please,* I whispered to myself.

"Ohhh… Joel, we aren't going anywhere, and maybe someday we will have a memory of you up on our walls," he told me.

"You'd do that?" I asked, looking up at him.

"Why wouldn't I? I did come and see you every month for the past seven-ish years. I'm not dying anytime soon, son, so you're stuck with me," he said in a matter-of-fact tone.

I didn't know what else to say except "thank you", so I just nodded, wiping away the tears that were forming again in the corners of my eyes.

Dufty moved from where he was sitting, his old bones creaking underneath him.

"I better go help Sofia with the dishes. Hope you sleep well. I'll see you tomorrow." He started toward the door, but then stopped, pausing before turning back. "A year or two after you were in prison, your dad contacted me."

I swallowed. "Do I want to know what he said?"

Dufty hesitated. "He said he was sorry… but never said anything about seeing you. He said he's happy with his life now."

I wasn't sure how to feel about that. "What about Mom?"

Dufty shook his head. "To this day, no one knows where she is... I'm sorry."

I nodded, and Dufty gave me a sad smile. He reached the door and flicked off the light. I still sat frozen, digesting my reality.

The news about Mom and Dad hurt for a second; for a second until I realized I had someone that truly cared about me. He was right in front of me, and I needed to let him know. I stood instantly, and before he could close the door fully, I pulled back at the handle and hugged him for the second time that day. I squeezed him so tight, afraid he was going to disappear. He felt so *real*. Everything was real.

My breathing hiccupped. He froze for a moment before wrapping his arms around me.

"Don't worry, son. I'm not going anywhere," Dufty said again into my ear before patting me twice on the back. He broke the hug and began walking down the stairs. "I'll see you tomorrow, bright n' early!" he yelled up from the bottom.

Even after what Dufty had told me about my parents, I couldn't stop smiling. I closed my door behind me and made my way over to my bed, landing on top of it. I barely finished taking off my shoes before I was asleep, too tired to worry about the possibility of restarting.

Chapter Forty-Five

Dufty wasn't kidding. A knock echoed into my room in the early hours of the next morning. I hardly flinched at the noise, until I heard the doorknob twist, his shadow only making it an inch into the room.

"Be ready in ten, *si*?" Dufty said in a very quiet, sleepy voice.

I twisted myself out of my blankets and saw a set of new clothes sitting on a chair in my room. I decided to put them on instead of the clothes I'd been wearing all day yesterday. I also found that they'd left a hairbrush and some deodorant next to the chair. They must have sneaked in while I was asleep, since I'm pretty sure I hadn't seen any of that before going to bed.

Even though Dufty was a fair bit shorter than me, his pants fit comfortably, leaving a little gap at my ankles. His shirt was actually too big, but that didn't matter. I just tucked it in.

I saw my hoodie off to the side, on the floor. I must have chucked it off in my sleep. I put it on, but then noticed an old Levi's denim jacket hanging on the hook on the back of my door. Considering it was probably before six in the morning, the fall chill would go straight through me, so I decided to put it on over the top.

Lastly, I chucked my shoes on and opened the door, making my way to the bathroom. I heard Dufty moving quietly downstairs, and I assumed Sofia was still asleep. I splashed some water on my face and put my head under the faucet, letting my hair get wet before using the hand towel to dry it. I parted it with the brush, but I didn't bother actually brushing it. It would look better natural.

I probably needed a haircut and a shave. We only got one haircut every three months in prison, sometimes every two if we were lucky. We couldn't do it ourselves for obvious reasons.

The wrinkles under my eyes made me look older than I was, I thought, noticing myself in the mirror. I honestly looked more like a forty-year-old.

I guessed I still looked the same, apart from the face full of stubble and my semi-long hair. Out of habit, I ruffled my hair and then rested my hands on my hips. I took a slow and controlled breath before opening the door and quietly making my way down the stairs.

Dufty was sitting at the table, tying his shoes. He stood up and grabbed his keys from the bowl on the table, throwing me an apple in the process. He gave me a small, sleepy smile before saying a quiet "come on" and nodding toward the front door.

Not more than ten minutes later, we pulled in behind Dufty's coffee bar, *Sunrise Sunset Roast*. I couldn't believe it was still running twenty-four hours every day. It was almost surreal to be here. Where I first met Dufty… where I was first given a chance.

"Come on, it's freezing in the car," Dufty said, opening his car door and quickly making his way to the coffee bar's back entrance.

I took another deep breath and followed him, jogging to catch up. I slipped through the door after Dufty, and I was welcomed by the kitchen's blasting heat. Dufty went ahead, greeting the cook with a pat on the shoulder.

I walked in a few steps, before bumping into a chair. Why was there a chair in the kitchen? No way. No, it couldn't be. He **never** moved the chair?

This, *this* was the same chair Livvie used to sit on. Had he left it there hoping we would come back one day?

The sink was right next to it, and I didn't think I was imagining it.

The stickers Livvie had stuck there as a kid were still on it. On this old musty, worn-down, brown plastic chair. I rested my hand on the back of it, my other hand running over the stickers. She sat here with me, every day. I backed away, looking at my sink. There was something new above it. On the wall was a laminated picture. I leaned over, getting as close as I could to it.

It was a picture of me when I was sixteen, wrapping my arms around Livvie who must have been twelve at the time. My hair was scruffy, *like it is now*, and I had some grime from the dishes stuck on my face. Livvie's beautiful blonde hair hugged her pale face, and her eyes were bright with surprise. They were always so bright. I was grinning, a goofy one. A memory pulled at me and I tried to look past it, but it devoured me...

"Come on, I need a photo of my two best dishwashers!" Dufty said, shoving a camera in Joel's face. Joel was tired from his day at school and couldn't be bothered fighting. Livvie was stuck in her library book.

Joel's thoughts were preoccupied with dinner, or rather their lack of it.

"Ughh, okay, sure," Joel said, taking his gloves off. He moved to the other side of Livvie without her noticing, and wrapped his arms around her, giving her a fright. In that moment, Dufty's camera flash went off.

"Joel! I wasn't ready! That's not fair!" Livvie whined, but she couldn't hold back her smile. Joel kissed her on the cheek and ruffled her hair which made her huff in annoyance. Dufty smiled at the photo he'd taken on his new digital camera. Joel had never seen one up close before.

Livvie stood to try ruffle Joel's hair, but he had several inches on her, and she could barely reach. He was too quick, and she was distracted. This was his time! He grabbed her book and quickly took out the bookmark, placing it on top.

"JOEL! YOU DID NOT! YOU'RE SO ANNOYING!" she yelled, already flicking through the pages like it was the end of the world.

"You still love me?" Joel asked cheekily, slipping his gloves back on to continue with the dishes.

"If you do that one more time, then no," Livvie said.

Joel laughed. Twelve-year-olds and their threats.

"I love you too," he replied, scooping up some bubbles and blowing them at her.

Livvie turned around with rage in her eyes, but she could never hold onto anger very long. Her lips were already quivering upwards. She dropped her book and walked over to his sink, dipping her hand in and grabbing her own bubbles. Without another thought, she smushed them into Joel's face, laughter erupting from her.

Livvie… I missed her.

I squeezed my eyes shut, afraid to look. *Please let me be in Dufty's kitchen, please, please, pleaseee.* I couldn't restart back in the station all over again.

"Joel?" Dufty asked, laying a hand on my shoulder.

I jumped, flinching and hitting my head on the shelf above the sink. My hands flew to my head, rubbing the spot that echoed pain. I turned around to Dufty

who was covering his mouth with his hands. What
was he trying to do... stop laughing?

His face was becoming redder every minute that
passed, causing me to chuckle, then full-on laugh. He
gasped for air and joined me. We were
uncontrollable. We couldn't stop for the longest time.
I even fell into Livvie's chair at one point.

A few dings on the bell at the front counter brought
us both back to our senses.

I joined Dufty out the front, dropping back into the
routine of serving customers. I found an abandoned
apron and tied it around my waist and made a fresh
pot of coffee, going around to each table, asking if
anyone wanted refills. After that, I wiped down all the
tables and chairs that weren't in use and gave the
floor a quick sweep. It was almost comforting, to be
able to clean. To be helpful.

Once I'd done that, I asked where Dufty needed me
next. He nodded toward the kitchen. I took the plates
ready for serving out to the customers before
returning to my sink. My scratched stainless-steel tub.

I found the gloves and dishwashing liquid under the
sink, where they'd always lived, and started with the
stack next to me. Dufty walked in, grabbing a few
fries, and leaned against the counter beside me.

"How come you've never installed a dishwasher,
Dufty?" I asked him, while scrubbing a plate. I'd
probably have to soak this one to be able to get all the
marks off it.

"Coz I always had someone do them," he replied, like it was a fact.

"What if you didn't?"

"Then, I'd have to install a dishwasher, wouldn't I?" He punched my shoulder, gently. "Another hour, *si?* Then we can head out," he told me before making his way back to the front counter.

*

"You ready to go, son?" Dufty asked, taking off his apron. He chucked it in the laundry bin and grabbed his car keys off the hook by the back door. It brought me out of my "dishes trance".

I shook my hands, then dried them, taking off my own apron and stretching out my back. The sink had always been annoyingly low. Maybe I would suggest moving it up.

Shutting the back door behind us, I shrugged on my jacket and hopped in the car next to Dufty. I had no idea where we were going, but I didn't mind in the slightest.

We pulled into a parking lot near the closest shopping center, and I was suspicious. He'd better not think that I needed anything more. I didn't.

"Dufty, no," I stopped him with my voice. He fell back into his seat, letting one of his legs hold the door open.

"Huh?"

"You aren't going to buy me anything. I don't need anything. Why are we here?" I asked, gesturing toward the stores.

"I'm not," he said.

"You're not?" I asked. The liar.

"Nope. You're going to pay me back," he said, getting out of the car very swiftly for someone who should be retired.

"Wait, Dufty," I called out to him, but he didn't stop this time. I got out of the car and shut my own door. "I really don't need anything else, please. It's okay." I could never repay him for what he'd already done for me, let alone adding this. He walked around to my side of the car and rested a hand on my shoulder.

"Let me help you. You are a son to me. And I would get my sons more clothes, more shoes, a phone, whatever they need. And if they want, they can pay me back. Nothing is stopping me from buying you something that you need." He paused and dropped his hand. He took a few steps backward. "And you need more clothes. You look like a clown in my pants, but at least the jacket looks good!" He turned around walking toward the shops.

I didn't deserve that man. I ran to catch up and followed him inside. I wrapped my arm over his shoulders, giving him a side hug before we entered the first store.

Chapter Forty-Six

I was in the process of doing a little spin for Dufty, showing off one of the new outfits he helped me choose, outside the men's changing rooms. I was filled with joy, having so much fun trying on whatever I wanted. I couldn't remember the last time I'd bought new clothes. Well, Dufty was buying them, but I'd said I would pay him back.

I was wearing these light denim-colored jeans that had ripped bottoms with a white basic tee tucked in. I was also wearing new black sneakers which looked smart as well as holding a gray hoodie in my hand.

None of this was fancy or anything, but I felt on top of the world. Dufty gave me a big thumbs-up and shooed me back into the changing room to try on another outfit.

After what felt like hours, we walked out with a bag stuffed full of our purchases. I got a few more boxer briefs, socks, couple of pairs of jeans, a pair of sweats, two pairs of sport shorts, some plain tees, a button-down, a few basic-colored hoodies, a beanie, a cap, casual sneakers, and dressy shoes. I also grabbed some toiletries, a notebook, and a cheap phone.

Dufty made me get a blazer, though I had no idea when I would wear it. He insisted it was "just in case" I needed it. That was all more than what I wanted to leave with, but Dufty kept throwing things into my basket.

Thankfully, I did convince him to get something for himself—matching slippers for him and Sofia.

"Sofiaaa! *Amore mio, ti ho preso qualcosa!*" Dufty called when he opened the front door. I dropped my bags by the stairs, following him into the kitchen where I could hear them talking back and forth. Sofia held the slippers up, eyeing them like they were solid gold. I leaned against the doorjamb, watching them interact. Dufty held his pair behind his back. He had a goofy grin plastered all over his face.

"Hello Sofia," I said, before they noticed me staring.

"Joel! Look at these! Did you help him pick these out?" she said with the biggest smile on her face. It wasn't like they were much, but I knew how she felt when it came to new things. You feel like a little kid when it doesn't happen often.

I laughed, shaking my head side to side. My hand rubbed across my lip before I tucked it into my back pocket.

"No, Dufty did it all by himself. It was allll him," I said, watching her turn back to him with even more surprise. And that's when he took out his pair from behind his back.

"Wait, why do you have two? *Quindi possiamo abbinarci?!* Matching pairs?!" Sofia practically screamed in excitement.

I hadn't thought it would be such a big deal, but apparently it was. She hopped up from her chair and threw her arms around Dufty, jumping up and down. She stopped and ran over to me, surprising me by throwing her arms around me and giving me a tight hug too.

"Did you convince him?" she demanded.

"Huh?"

"You must have," she said, leaning away from me now, giving me a serious look.

"I had no input," I told her.

"*Promettere?* Promise?" she raised her eyebrow.

"Promise." I nodded my head firmly, and she let go of me, running back to Dufty who was smiling ear to ear. She kicked off her shoes and sat down putting on her slippers like she couldn't do it fast enough.

"*Indossate il vostro,*" she told Dufty, hitting his shin. He obediently kicked his shoes off and put his slippers on too.

"She's freaking out because—" Dufty started, but Sofia hit his middle, shutting him up.

"I am not freaking out, Joel. He just never does this. I try to get him to wear matching Christmas sweaters with me every year and he refuses, *la capra testarda!*" she said, with fire lacing her tone.

I couldn't help but laugh. The way she switched from English to Italian so quickly was insane. She stared daggers into me, which only made me laugh more. Her stare didn't last long, as she broke into laughter too. Dufty followed soon after. Then the whole kitchen turned into a room full of headless chickens.

*

An hour later, the laughter had passed, and I had to get out of there. I retreated upstairs with all my new stuff and dropped it on my bed. I hadn't noticed the time, but it was only midday, meaning we must have only covered the morning shift at the coffee bar.

I kind of just lay there on my bed surrounded by my new stuff until I heard a knock on my door. It wasn't closed.

"You ready to go?" Dufty asked. I sat up, ruffling my hair in a sleepy daze. I hadn't fallen asleep, but tiredness pulled at me now.

"Where to now?" I asked.

"You said you'd pay me back, right, or did I hear that wrong?" he said with a smile.

"Oh yeah... Yeah!" I said, standing and grabbing a beanie out of one of the bags, and my jacket which was lying next to me.

We arrived at the coffee bar not long after, and we both jumped straight into our routines. He served customers, chatting with them like they were lifelong friends, and I cleaned, topped up coffees and smiled politely at everyone. Then I went back to my dishes and did them for a couple of hours, until Dufty tapped me on the shoulder.

"You gonna have a break soon, son?" Dufty asked, pulling me from the never-ending dishes. My back **ached**.

"If you want me to, boss," I said, already taking off my gloves and apron.

"Sounds like you've already decided." Dufty patted me on the shoulder and left me a burger wrapped up on the counter.

"Thanks. I think I'll head out on a walk. To get some fresh air," I said, catching him before he went through the kitchen door.

"Okay, well, you have half an hour, but if you need more time, I'll be going home at six," he said before walking through the door.

"Thanks. Don't worry, I know where you live!" I yelled back at him, shrugging my jacket on and walking out the back with the burger in tow.

I didn't really have any destination in mind, I just felt like a wander around my old neighborhood. So that's what I did; I just kept walking toward it.

I knew I probably should've gone back to Dufty's after half an hour, but I could feel something pulling me outside, and I couldn't ignore it.

The sky was clouded and backlit by the sun. Surprisingly, it hadn't started to rain yet. The air did have a fall crispness to it, which I preferred anyway. It would probably get dark in a few hours' time.

Before I realized it, I felt something pulling me down my old street, then up my old steps, making me come face to face with my old front door. An eviction notice was taped onto it, looking like it had been there for *years*. I wasn't surprised to see it.

I went to open it, when I stopped. I didn't live there anymore. Mom obviously didn't live here anymore. Was she even alive? Was I about to scare a bunch of strangers?

I took a few steps back, hitting the railing. In all honesty, this whole apartment block looked abandoned, just a few people using it as temporary shelter. I used to use this place as some sort of shelter. After Livvie died, I stopped calling it *home*. It was just a roof, with a bed, and some protection from the New York weather.

"Ahh, crab," I mumbled, stepping forward and knocking on the door. Oh well, I'd done it now.

I waited a minute for a reply, then another, and then another. Still nothing. Cautiously, I twisted the knob and pushed the door in. A click echoed from the lock, sounding stiff. I pushed the door a little harder, and its hinges cried out to me.

I put one foot in and then another, and before I knew it, I was inside. I was *home.* And *home* looked like a war zone. What had happened here?

If she was evicted, the owner must've thought it was a too big a job to clean up for someone new to move in.

Everything that had been on the walls, and I mean *everything*, had been thrown onto the floor. The kitchen cabinets had been smashed into pieces, glass everywhere. Picture frames had been torn apart, an old tv had been kicked in, and there were stains on the couch, the walls, and the floor. It was *too much.* ***It was too much.***

I turned around, running back out the door and gripped the railing. My heart raced, and déjà vu filled me. It felt almost exactly the same as it had all those years ago at the train station… *was I about to restart?*

I looked down at the place I used to keep my bike, our escape route tore through my mind. I wanted to leave, to escape.

"No! Not anymore! I'm not afraid of you!" I yelled, turning around and storming back inside. I could hear my heart drum out.

This time, I noticed the caution tape blocking off the hallway. I stepped over the broken cupboards and ducked under the tape, making my way down the hallway.

I called out, in case anyone was down there, and walked straight past mine and Livvie's room. I had to check Mom's room first. I stood outside her door. There was faded yellow caution tape stuck all over it, yelling at me, warning me. I pushed the door open anyway.

"Mom…?"

No answer. I didn't expect one, but I couldn't help myself. A smell so potent hit me in the face, making

me take a few steps back. I knocked into her dresser
and spun around. Half the drawers were missing,
most of them thrown around the room.

Rags of old clothes, mice droppings, blood,
syringes, and condom wrappers were the most
common things in sight.

Stepping around the old bed frame, which was half
broken, the mattress slipped down on what was
Mom's side of the bed.

What looked like a few old needles and hundreds of
little pouches from the heroin she took were scattered
all over the floor and all over her bedside table. I took
another step forward, covering my hand with my
sleeve to brush away some trash so I could open the
bedside table drawer.

The first thing that greeted me was a picture of all
four of us on top of her old Bible. I remembered her
reading from that when I was little, before Livvie was
born. After that, she seemed to have run out of time.

Even though the mattress was probably infested
with something, I sat down on her side, reaching into
the drawer, and taking out the Bible and photo. I
wiped both on my hoodie, the dirty dust spreading
across my clothes.

We all looked so young and happy in the picture. I'd
only just turned five, Livvie was about one, and Mom
and Dad actually still looked happy, apart from the
big bags under their eyes.

I put the photo to the side and picked up the Bible.
Skimming the pages, I found what I thought was a

271

bookmark. On inspection, it was Mom's gold necklace with her wedding and engagement ring on it, and a piece of paper folded in half.

Taking a closer look at Mom's rings, I moved the Bible to my side, sliding the photo inside the front cover, exchanging it for the piece of paper. Flicking it open, I gasped.

It was a hand-written letter, addressed to me and Livvie. Mom wrote us a letter? I closed it. I didn't know if I could read that right now. I didn't even know how it was still there.

Slipping the letter back in the Bible with the photo, I put Mom's necklace on so I didn't lose it. Standing, I made my way out of her room without looking back.

My old bedroom door stopped me next. It was closed too, but there wasn't any caution tape on it. I twisted the handle gently, opening it. I let it fall in, let the inside show itself.

It was almost as we'd left it. Livvie's Dory comforter was ripped in a few areas, Dory's face torn in two. My bed was gone, but Livvie's drawings were still taped to the walls. Our drawers looked ransacked; our clothes thrown on the floor. I stepped inside the room, and that's when I saw it. Massive black letters scrawled across the wall behind the door. They looked suspiciously like dried blood...

"WHERE ARE YOU???"

The letters were shaky, looking like they'd been painted in a panic. Was this why the place was tipped upside down? Had Mom been looking for us? How long had this been painted on the wall? I hadn't been here since I was eighteen...

I took a few steps back. I felt like this place was a ticking timebomb, about to go off... and it felt like my neck was in a noose, tightening quickly. I needed to get out of here.

Turning around, I grabbed some drawings off the walls, one of Livvie's old teddies, and my old school bag. I stuffed everything inside, then grabbed her pillow, which was surprisingly still clean-ish. Zipping up my bag, I threw it on my back in a rush like I used to, and hauled ash out of there.

I slammed the front door behind me and ran down the stairs, slipping down the last two, the railing just catching me. Pushing myself back up, I brushed off my pants and rolled my shoulders before setting off down the road without looking back.

I turned down roads from memory, making my way closer to Dufty's house. I finally slowed my pace after about ten minutes of urgent running. I made myself breathe, slowing everything down. The air was sharper than I remembered, and the sun looked like it was almost about to set. I hadn't realized how long I'd been in the old apartment. Brooklyn was not a safe place at night, not even for a twenty-six-year-old that had won a few fights in prison. This thought helped me get a move on, and I couldn't help but bounce into a jog.

*

Trudging up the steps to Dufty's house, I came face to face with the doorbell. They were going to be so mad. I hadn't told them anything. They'd be worried. They'd throw me out. I should have called or texted.

"Joel…?" Sofia's voice brought me back. She held the door open, looking up at me, worry consuming her face. "Come in, come in, you're freezing," she said, pulling me inside, exactly the same way she had the day before. She closed the door behind us. How had she known I was outside? I never knocked… Maybe she was waiting for me?

"I'm sorry," was all I could manage. This was not what I thought my first full day out of prison would be like.

"Don't be silly, go sit down. I'm going to call Dufty, so he doesn't wait for you," she said, walking away to get the home phone from the wall in the kitchen. I was glad she'd decided that now wasn't the time to go full Italian on my dumb ash.

I took a seat on the couch, feeling exhausted. I didn't know what I was thinking, going back there. I could feel all the memories fresh in my mind. It was as if I'd put up an invisible wall once Livvie died, and I never let myself back there again.

But I must have known I needed to. I hadn't wanted to until I was there, looking at my old door. I knew I had to see it if I was going to fully heal.

"You alright, Joel?" Sofia asked, slipping silently into the room and taking a seat next to me.

"Yeah, yeah, thanks, Sofia," I said, my head still hanging low. I couldn't look at her.

"You know, I can tell when people lie to me. It's one of my gifts I got when I became a mother. The amount of times my little *mascalzoni* lied to me almost made me a master of interpretation. Joel, I know you're still hurting, and when you're ready to talk about it, I'm here." Sofia grabbed my hand off my lap and held it with both of hers.

I couldn't help it, I let myself cry. I couldn't be strong anymore. Hurt wrapped around my heart, squeezing it, making the tears uncontrollable. I leaned over to Sofia, who welcomed me, wrapping her arms around as much of me as she could. She didn't say another word. She just let me cry and never told me once to stop.

I bawled like a baby, but I needed to. I didn't even realize Dufty slipped in and began making dinner before I'd finished. I felt completely and utterly exhausted, but eventually my tears dried up. I didn't think I would be able to sit through dinner with them.

Moving out of Sofia's arms, I noticed that I was still wearing my backpack. She never even asked me about it.

Sofia gave me a sad smile and stood up, straightening out her clothes. Her shirt now had a big wet patch where my tears had decided to pool. I gave her a sad smile in return and stood with her, finally taking my beanie off.

"I think Dufty has just about finished dinner. Let's go see?" she asked, already walking off. She glanced back to make sure I was following. I met them both, stopping at the kitchen doorjamb, leaning into the spot I'd made earlier that day.

"If it's okay, I'm going to head upstairs and have a shower and then sleep. I'm exhausted. I'm sorry." I couldn't be bothered making another excuse. Sofia nodded her understanding, and Dufty looked up from what he was doing.

"That's absolutely fine, Joel. We will leave you a plate, just in case you get hungry," he said without an inch of annoyance.

"Thank you. Are we catching the breakfast shift tomorrow again?"

"If you'd like?" Dufty asked, sounding a little hesitant.

"Yes. Knock on my door?" I asked him.

"Will do," he said, nodding. His gaze went to Sofia for a second, as she took a seat next to him at the table.

"Thank you both again. Goodnight," I said, pushing off the doorjamb.

"Goodnight, son," Dufty said, getting right back to whatever he was working on.

I grabbed Livvie's pillow from where I'd dropped it by the stairs and took the creaky steps one at a time, fighting my exhaustion.

Once I reached the top, I dropped my bag and her pillow on my bed with all my other stuff. Grabbing out a new pair of boxers and a shirt, I went to the bathroom for a shower.

I didn't take long in there, just enough time to get clean. I got changed before heading back to my room and moved my bags off my bed, promising myself I'd begin sorting those out the next day. I didn't think Sofia would be very happy if I continued to live out of plastic bags.

I hopped into bed, and to my surprise it was warm. Sofia must have switched on the electric blanket while I was in the shower. *Once a mother, always a mother…*

Mom's letter! I sprung back out of bed and unzipped my bag, taking the Bible out carefully. I rested it on my bedside table, and took out the photo and letter. I hadn't even noticed that I was still wearing Mom's necklace around my neck…

I looked around the room and walked over to the set of drawers, hoping to find a free photo frame. There was one in the second drawer I opened. Undoing the back, I slipped my photo in, placing it on the bedside table.

It would probably be best if I didn't wear my mom's necklace to bed, so I took that off, letting it hang over the frame.

Climbing back under the covers and getting comfortable, I grabbed Mom's letter out of her Bible with shaky hands. I had no idea what I was about to read. The paper was wrinkled and smudged in places. It looked about ten years old.

277

Before I changed my mind, I unfolded it quickly but carefully, letting my eyes scan the page.

Dear Olivia and my Joel,

I'm sorry. I'm not sure what else I should say, really. I have been a horrible mother. I don't know what happened. It was like I had this little bug in me ever since I was born and then once I had Olivia, it became active. It just started eating away at me and I couldn't stop it. I only fed it, but I fed it everything, all of me.

I assume if you ever read this, that I am too far gone. I guess I'm writing this already knowing that's the path I'm going down.

You two are great. You are the best human beings I know. Olivia, I'm sorry I could never show you my love. I birthed you for heaven's sake, I'm a monster. I do have memories when you'd light up my life for short bursts, mostly because your hair was so blonde, it was almost blinding when the sun hit it, like my momma's was. I hope you'll find all the happiness you deserve. Olivia, my peace.

Joel, my boy. I loved you from the moment I saw you. We had a blast, you and I. You could always make me laugh, you always forgave, you're always smiling, my bright-eyed boy. I am so sorry I made you grow up faster than you should have. Thank you for trying to take care of me and for always taking care of your sister. You are the best brother. Olivia is so lucky to have you. You're going to make a great husband and an even better dad one day. You have so much love in you, and I hope it does the opposite for you than it has done to me. I hope it'll make you stronger.

Love, Mom

P.S. I always hear you two crawl in and out of the house and sometimes I want to walk into your room and give you two a hug, knowing that you're safe, but I always knew it would be better to leave you be than to scare you more...

Woah. I read it again, and then again, and I couldn't help but read it for a fourth time.

That was the mom I knew when I was little—the one with the kind words, the one that wanted to know where I was all the time as I ran around a playground. She was still in there. She was still inside the monster she became; the one she knew she was becoming when writing her letter.

It was like she *had to* write that and get that off her chest before she completely gave up on herself. And the worst part was that she didn't even know Livvie had died. I never told her. I tried to suck up the courage the day after it happened, but she was away with the fairies, and I walked out of her room.

I folded the letter back up and slid it inside her Bible. I turned onto my back and looked up at the ceiling. I was only going to keep the good memories of her—of Mom.

She still loved us, even when she was becoming a different person, a person even she couldn't recognize in the mirror. If I was being honest with myself, I still loved her. And I always would.

I turned back to my bedside table, looking at the picture of the four of us. Dad's hair flopped all over his forehead, smiling wide, dimples on either side, looking straight into the camera lens. One arm was around Mom's shoulders. Mom with her sunhat on, her nose and cheeks sprinkled with freckles, her eyes happy but tired. Her arms were around me and Livvie. You could tell her smile was directed down at me, and I was smiling straight back up at her with a whole lot of love. And baby Livvie was quietly asleep in my little arms, wrapped up tight in a starry, moleskin blanket. Her little hands just popped over the edge, trying to escape. Livvie, my little present.

Chapter Forty-Seven

November 1ˢᵗ, 2016
One week later

Nothing much changed. My days kept going. I went to work with Dufty every day, starting at about four in the morning, staying until about eleven. We would come back for lunch and a quick nap, then go back at one in the afternoon until about six, to come home for dinner.

Sofia, Dufty and I would talk about our days over dinner, then do the dishes and then get ready for bed. It became a routine, and I didn't mind one bit.

Dufty and Sofia let me help around the house a little more—my one week free of chores had finished, so I was happily helping out in any way I could.

Neither Dufty nor Sofia brought up what happened the day I went back to my old house. They didn't even ask where I got my bag or Livvie's pillow, and if they noticed my mom's necklace around my neck, they pretended they didn't.

I think they both came to the same conclusion on where I was that evening. They definitely would have figured it out if they looked in my room, which had all of the *"evidence"* sitting around.

Saturday was my day off. Dufty and Sofia were taking a drive out to Long Island to see their granddaughter, which would be nice for them. They asked whether I wanted to come with them, but I declined. I didn't want to be more of a burden than I already was.

I heard them leave around seven. Three hours later, I was still lying in bed, procrastinating. *Procrastinating what?* I asked myself. I didn't have anywhere to be or anything to do. I still felt like I needed to get up and actually enjoy my day off.

Grabbing some clothes, which now lived in *my* drawers, I took them to the bathroom. I had a shower to wake myself up. I let the water run over my head, and I just stood there, letting myself soak up the warmth.

I started to trace the tiles with my fingers. They were a strange bluey green color, checkered with a white tile. The greeny color brought a sense of familiarity, but I couldn't put a finger on why that was. I let my mind wander for the rest of my shower, and once I was done, I turned it off and pushed the curtain open, stepping out onto the bath mat.

Drying myself quickly, I got changed and put some black jeans on, a button-down shirt, and chucked a green hoodie over the top. I hung my towel on the rack and walked back to my room to grab some socks and my shoes. Spraying on some cologne, I attempted to brush through my hair but gave up. Instead, I moved it around with my hands, letting it flop to the sides and a little over my forehead. Ahh well, scruffy it was then.

I walked back into the bathroom, wiping an area in the mirror to see my reflection. I should have shaved but it was only a few days of stubble. No one was going to notice. I wasn't trying to impress anyone either.

My eye bags were pretty dark, and my wrinkles were coming through. I looked like my dad. What was I expecting? I was my dad's child. I was basically an *old man*, living with his "parents".

"Oh well," I sighed, closing the door behind me, and making my way down the stairs. Walking into the kitchen, I grabbed an apple, noticing a little note on the table.

'Joel, there's leftovers in the fridge. Have a good day. We are going to be late tonight! Don't wait up! – Sofia & Dufty'

Short and sweet. *Nice.* I could have figured that all out for myself, but it was nice of Sofia to tell me. They also could have texted, but when I thought about it, my phone was still somewhere upstairs, charging.

I opened their back door and went out into their little garden. Heading for the shed, I hoped to find a bike or something, so I didn't have to walk everywhere. The weather wasn't too bad, though, a bit overcast with a slight chill in the air. The sun peeked out behind the clouds every now and again, which was nice.

I popped the last of the apple into my mouth, and thankfully found the door to the shed unlocked. Sliding it open, I let the daylight pour in. In the back corner, it looked like there was a bike. I reached over and grabbed the handlebars, hauling it up and out of the shed.

"No way," I said around the apple in my mouth. It was *my* bike. Dufty had my bike this entire time? *Why?* I just assumed it got picked up and dropped off at the dump, or stolen, but Dufty must have picked it up from the station.

To my surprise, the tires still had air in them, and it looked like it was in working condition. Man, the memories that bike had.

I shook my head and rolled my bike toward the back door, leaning it carefully on a wall inside before going back and shutting up the shed.

I ran back upstairs and grabbed my bag, my denim jacket, and my phone before running back down to the kitchen. I grabbed some snacks and some cash, which I knew they wouldn't mind me using. It was harder than you might think to open a bank account when you'd been in prison, mostly because I hadn't had a home address for seven years.

I also filled up a water bottle and chucked everything in my bag. Rolling my bike toward the front door, I found a spare key and attached it to my belt loop along the way.

I locked the door behind me, then carried my bike down the steps. I adjusted the seat to a higher position and bent the handlebars backwards a little before swinging my leg over and taking off down the road. I didn't really have anywhere in mind; I was just going to ride in the direction the bike took me.

*

An hour or so later, I was sticky with sweat. I'd made it to central New York, where everything was bustling with people and traffic. The noise was disorienting, and I could no longer concentrate. I hopped off my bike and pushed it through the crowds. Everything about the city brought back memories, and it had hardly changed. It felt like I was here just yesterday...

I couldn't help it, I'd somehow biked to Grand Central Station. The color of the tiles in the bathroom clicked in my brain, reminding me of the celestial ceiling in the station. It was Livvie's favorite thing.

I stopped just outside of the building and looked up at it. I hadn't considered the idea that being here might make me restart... Surely not. I didn't even think about going in; I was not ready for that. I didn't know if I'd ever be ready.

I kind of gaped at it for a few minutes. This magnificent building was the start of my path of recovery. This place held so many memories, memories only I had experienced. No one else would believe me if I told them what actually happened. I had tried, but it had only made people think I was unwell. I probably would have been thrown into a psychiatric hospital next if I tried to tell someone now. I did not want that to happen.

Taking a few steps back, I slowly made space between me and the station, feeling like I could breathe properly again. Walking further down the sidewalk, I let people push me forward until I was around the corner. I was thankful for the commuters; they were helping me break my connection with the station.

I looked up and saw a coffeehouse sign; it was called "Starry Drinks". It caught my attention, and I moved out of the ongoing crowd. I chained my bike to one of the bike stands outside, and repositioned my bag. Pushing my hair back out of my eyes, I opened the door to the cafe.

It was lit with fairy lights which covered the navy blue painted ceiling. It was like the night sky. The place bustled with people who were seated in every available chair. I could feel the energy inside. It was happy; people were chatting, laughing, and so many smiles were being shared.

I waited in line until it was my time to order, and once I reached the counter, I noticed that everything was star-shaped, or tried to be star-shaped. Even the workers were wearing these silver star-shaped aprons which looked so silly, it almost made me giggle. At least the owner of the place had fully committed to their theme.

"You ready to order, sir?" the girl behind the cash register asked. The tag on her apron told me her name was Becky.

"Uh, yes, yes," I said, looking at their star-themed menu board. "Can I have the Cold Starry Night please? That's an iced coffee, right?" I asked her.

Her eyes widened in surprise. "Shh, don't tell the other customers that's all it is. You'll ruin the effect!" she said quickly, teasing me.

"Oh, oops. I can't wait to try it. I've always wanted to know what the night tasted like..." I replied, embarrassment flaring up in me.

Becky giggled, and behind me, another customer also laughed quietly.

"One Cold Starry Night coming up. That'll be five dollars and seventy-five cents, please," she said.

I handed over a ten-dollar note and told her to keep the change. I moved out of the line to wait for my drink.

It didn't take long at all, which was nice. I'd been starting to feel a little claustrophobic as more and more people tried to squeeze inside. I made my way to the counter, saying a quick thanks to Becky, and then squeezed back through everyone, being as careful as I could not to spill my drink.

Finally, I popped out the door. It was, thankfully, quieter outside than it was before. I strolled over to my bike and leaned against the wall, taking a sip. It was literally just an iced coffee. It didn't *take* me anywhere... It wasn't bad, though.

The cup was the best part. There were a whole lot of little stars drawn above a horizon that wrapped around the whole cup. It was a cool effect.

Taking another sip, I looked up toward the sky. It'd cleared up, letting the blue seep through the gaps in the clouds. It would be amazing if we could see stars in the daytime too, but then I guess that wouldn't make stars as special...

"Whatcha looking at?" a girl's voice bumped into me, at the same time as her shoulder.

My eyes whipped down. It couldn't be...

It was her.

She looked older, but in a good way. Her hair still flowed over her shoulders, but this time it was tucked into a long ponytail. Her honey eyes looked at me then up to the sky. She was smiling, one side curved up more than the other, making her look a little... *goofy*. She wore a long brownish plaid skirt, a white long-sleeved shirt tucked in with a dark denim jacket. She wore black boots... *the same ones?* She held a drink covered in stars... Was she the customer behind me who'd laughed?

"You know, you're the first person I've seen looking up." She brought her gaze down from the sky, locking eyes with me. Those honey eyes were melting my heart, melting my soul. I'd never felt myself fall for someone so fast. *Fall for someone so fast,* **again.**

"Do you believe in love at first sight?" I blurted out. I almost smacked myself. What was I thinking?

"Hmm… depends," she said, still looking at me. She took a sip from her drink.

"On?" I asked gingerly.

"If they are looking at the sky or not," she said with a smile. That smile. That smile made me weak in the knees.

"Would you believe me if I told you we've met before?" I asked.

This time she fully turned toward me. She was almost a head shorter than me; the perfect height for giving her forehead kisses…

"If you had, then wouldn't it be love at second sight?" she asked.

"I guess you're right…" I said, barely containing my smile.

"I guess I am." She was still looking at me with curiosity, like she was trying to recognize me.

"Joel," I said, holding my free hand out for her to shake. She glanced at it before slipping her hand into mine. It fitted perfectly. Heat rose in her cheeks. Was she feeling the same way I was?

"Ella. Where you off to, lover boy?" she asked, without even thinking twice. Did she know who I was? Did she remember? Surely not... Could it be possible?

"Joel?" she asked me again. Her eyes searched mine, concern absorbing her happiness. *No, no, **no.*** Was this real?

This. Was. Real.

"Uh... I have no set destination in mind. Do you... would you like to—"

"Yes. Yes, I would," she said, cutting me off.

"You don't even know what I was going to say."

"Well, I hope I've assumed right, then," she said, bumping her shoulder into mine again.

"Are you sure?" I asked hesitantly. She didn't even know me.

"Joel, I feel something in my gut that's telling me to hang out with you, that I know you even though I don't think I've ever seen you before in my life. So yes, I'm sure, as long as you don't turn out to be an axe murderer or something," she said, with an honesty that made me take a step back.

"You're something else, you know that? By the way, I'm not an axe murderer," I assured her, and started to chuckle. Someday, I would have to tell her the whole story, how in the past I did blow myself up, and a bunch of strangers... but technically I'm not an axe murderer.

"Good." Ella laughed with me.

I walked over to my bike and unchained it, quickly finishing my drink. Ella followed my lead, looking from me to my bike a few times. I could see her nerves building.

"Don't worry, my sister and I rode this bike everywhere. You'll be perfectly safe," I said, swinging my leg over the seat.

She still looked nervous but nodded anyway. She had so much trust in me already, and I was basically a complete stranger. The circumstances couldn't have been weirder.

She positioned herself onto my handlebars, her feet standing on the bike pegs. Her hands squeezed the handle bars so tight, they started to turn white.

"You ready?" I whispered in her ear.

"Okay," she said, nodding at the same time. I set us off, already falling back into routine. Ella let out a little squeal, but after a few minutes I could see her relax as I weaved us through people and other obstacles.

Epilogue

Today was our fifth wedding anniversary, and I couldn't be happier. Things had gone so smoothly that for a while, I was sure I was bound to restart. Every morning after waking up, I whispered a quiet thanks to the world.

I proposed to Ella with my mom's ring about six months into dating and then married her about two months later, thanks to her and Sofia's magical organizing skills. I was head over heels for her and saying *"I do"* would forever be one of the happiest days in my life. I was unbelievably lucky to have her.

I told her everything and surprisingly she accepted me for who I was and helped me be a better person with every new day. It was funny because I never believed that your significant other brought out the best in you until I met Ella... again.

I continued to work at Dufty's for another two years after getting married before I found the courage to suggest that Dufty should sell his business. He and

Sofia were actually all for the idea, and they couldn't wait to retire and hand me the ropes.

We sold Dufty's twenty-four-hour coffee bar and bought a small place near Grand Central Station. I put hours into the new coffee bar, and I was so proud of what I had achieved. I named it *"Dufty's"* as a little tribute to the old man himself.

When you walked through the door, the first thing you noticed was the ceiling. I hired someone to paint a replica of the celestial ceiling from the train station, and then I added little lights as stars everywhere.

I also wanted it to be a place of refuge and familiarity, so I built a floor-to-ceiling bookcase that covered an entire wall. People could freely browse, grab any book they wanted and read it while they dined or at it home.

However, there was a twist, which Ella came up with. Customers had to promise to bring a book to exchange the next time they came in. Whenever I was in the coffee bar, I loved watching complete strangers converse about books they both had read. It was the most interesting thing.

On one of the other walls, I hung up my old bike. I framed my story around it, just like Sofia and Dufty's kitchen walls. I added newspaper clippings, photos, and other little memories which had helped me get to where I was now.

Instead of wooden tables and chairs, I had beanbags and couches so people could make themselves comfortable and stay as long as they needed.

Lastly, following in Dufty's footsteps, I decided that I'd never install a dishwasher. I wanted to be that person to give someone a chance, like Dufty had done for me.

Life couldn't possibly have been better. Well... actually, it was about to get *a whole lot* better, as we prepared to welcome a little girl into the world.

We already had a name picked out and everything. Her name was going to be **Dahlia Elaine Lewis**. Named after a bold and beautiful valley flower that blooms in the late summer, and Elaine was Livvie's middle name.

My story had made me who I was, and I couldn't be prouder. I freely told people about my struggles, but I always put the emphasis on how I kept trying, and how I had found hope in my past.

Most nights after I arrived home from work, I liked to take some time outside looking up at the stars, and sometimes Ella joined me. However, lately it had gotten a bit hard for her to lie down on the ground, since she was about to give birth soon.

I would tell Livvie about my day, letting her live through me, since she would always be a part of my life. I told her every day how I wished she was here; how I wished she could become an aunty, how I wished she was living life with me and not just through me. But mostly, I wished—I hoped—I was making her proud. I would always keep trying to be and do the best I could.

For her. For Ella. For Dufty and Sofia. For Mom. For me. And for my little baby girl, that would no doubt have the brightest eyes, just like her aunty.

The Stars Aren't Ready Playlist

Life, I'm over you : **Zevia**
Lonely : **Imagine Dragons**
Listen before I go : **Billie Eilish**
Burn : **David Kushner**
Fix You : **Coldplay**
The Loneliest : **Måneskin**
In The Stars : **Benson Boone**
Heal : **Tom Odell**
Medicine : **The Wild Youth**
Let Her Go : **Passenger** — this song hits hard in Chapter 26
Its Ok : **Imagine Dragons**
The Long & Winding Road : **Himesh Patel**
Little Freak : **Harry Styles**
I Wanna Love Somebody : **We Three**
I Was Made For Lovin' You : **Kiss**
Dancing in the sky : **Kristen Cruz**
I'm Still Standing : **Elton John**

Resources

If you're a victim of child abuse/abandonment, suffering from depression/suicidal thoughts or drug usage, or you know someone who could use any assistance in finding help, please call one of the helplines listed below.

NEW ZEALAND
Oranga Tamariki line – 0508 326 459
Need to talk line – 1737 (call or message)
Youthline – 0800 376 633
Hey Bro Helpline – 0800 439 276

If you or someone you know needs urgent care (even if you're not sure) please call 111

AUSTRALIA
Kids Helpline – 1800 55 1800
Lifeline – 13 11 14
eheadspace Line – 1800 650 890
Family Drug Support Line – 1300 368 186

If you or someone you know needs urgent care (even if you're not sure) please call 000

UNITED STATES
Childhelp Line – 1800 422 4453

National Suicide and Crisis Lifeline – 988
National Domestic Violence Hotline – 800 799 7233
Substance abuse and Mental Health Helpline – 800 662 4357

If you or someone you know needs urgent care (even if you're not sure) please call 911

UNITED KINGDOM
National Suicide Prevention Helpline – 0800 689 5652
Samaritans Line – 116 123
Childline – 0800 1111
NSPCC Helpline – 0808 800 5000

If you or someone you know needs urgent care (even if you're not sure) please call 999

If these helplines don't apply to you, please google your national helpline or website to find assistance. It's okay to reach out for help, to talk. You are not being a burden.

Remember, you're valued, you're strong and you are irreplaceable.

Acknowledgments

This book was honestly one of the most confusing things I've written—you should see the number of notes surrounding my laptop right now. It's absolute chaos—but so is this book… I'm not sure why I decided to play with the idea of "time" and what death could potentially be like. And wow, I don't think I'll ever write something so complicated again.

I want to give you a little insight into the amount of research I do when I write, something you've probably noticed with all the New York facts I've slipped in throughout this book. ANYWAY, I'm rambling— something I do when I'm excited.

So, I think the main character names in books are important and should be chosen on purpose. I was going to name Joel's baby girl "Summer" after his mom, but I realized it didn't work since his mom wasn't always the greatest. That's when I thought of "Dahlia". A flower. A bold, bright and beautiful flower that creates a little link to my other book, *"The Butterfly Sanctuary"*.

But, the real reason why I liked it was because it meant kindness and commitment but also, a Dahlia can flower until late autumn which ties them to be steadfast and well, I just think that's a pretty special flower.

If I could use one word to describe my book, *"The Stars Aren't Ready",* it would be hope—something everyone needs a little bit of. I know I covered some big topics throughout this book, but that's only because I don't want them to be swept under the rug anymore. Taking your life or even attempting to should be talked about more often; people shouldn't think that the whole topic is seen as some sort of "curse". If you are ever feeling how Joel felt throughout my book, please seek the resources or talk to someone you trust.

I'd like to give my warmest thanks to everyone who helped me with publishing my SECOND book—

Helen Fletcher – for editing my second book! After working with you on my first, I couldn't think of anyone else who I would rather work with. I cannot thank you enough. You were so quick to answer all my questions and you always make everything so clear. I feel like I have created a story that is ten times better than what I started with, and I thank you for helping me with that.

Ruth Baines – for taking time out of your teaching schedule to do my first proofread of my book; your help means the world to me.

Victoria McPherson – for doing my final proofread! After your proofread, I knew I could confidently publish my book. Thank you for all the little comments you left, I really take note of them and they help me become a better writer.

Jeanne – for creating my technical little flip clock drawings at the top right corner; you brought my vision to life, and I love it!

Kelly Carter – for taking all my crazy ideas and creating the perfect cover, thank you, thank you, thank you! Also, sorry for being an indecisive pain, sometimes my ideas overwhelm me!

Monroe Brackey & Lynda Tomalin – for BETA reading my book, you guys really made me feel confident about everything I've written!

Lastly, I would like to thank everyone reading my book right now. It means the world that my 'art' is out there, that I'm living my dream—well at least trying to pursue it. ·

This book was a rollercoaster of emotions so hopefully you ended up in happy tears like I did when I read my epilogue out loud. Something about finishing writing a book gets me every time, and I'm just a blubbery mess, so I apologize if you are too, but again thank you for giving *"The Stars Aren't Ready"* a go!

Thank you again for reading *"**The Stars Aren't Ready"**.* If you'd like to leave a review (I would LOVE to hear your thoughts), please share it on the website you purchased a copy of my book on, through Goodreads by simply typing in the title, or by finding me on Instagram and tagging me in your review @grp.books

You can also contact me by sending me an email at grp.books.co@gmail.com

Thanks!

CPSIA information can be obtained
at www.ICGtesting.com
Printed in the USA
BVHW030728180123
656507BV00011B/51